The revenge is mine!

Gert van Jaarsveld

Read half of this book for free online in Stories magazine

https://storymagazine.home.blog

ISBN: 9798825952178

CONTENTS

1.   HANNES.

The light is almost too bright for his eyes accustomed to the artificial light inside the jail. Somehow, he can't believe his eyes. Trees across the street, the late afternoon sun bright on the green leaves and shades against the wall behind them. Even the ugly, grey brick wall is breathtakingly beautiful. The pavement is a purple carpet covered with jacaranda flowers.

He looks up and down the street but all is quiet. Only a blue delivery van is lazily coming down the street.

It is difficult to get his mind around the expectation he had about his freedom. The unreality that instantly changed to reality fogs his mind. He didn't associate his freedom with pavements and walls. Nor with jacarandas and shades. His freedom was bright like a star. It was white. It was open. Yes, his freedom was a dream, an emotion, not bricks and colour and trees.

He will have to get used to his release.

Slowly, the reality overwhelms him. He starts to bind his freedom to the existence of the things he sees. Slowly he becomes overwhelmed by experiences other than cells, jail walls, cramped spaces, limited movement.

He is out of jail!

Then it washes through him. Free, free, free! After eight years, really free! Now it makes even more sense to him that he rejected parole. His thoughts wander over the trees, the walls, the street, even the wide world. A future? You make your own future. For that, you sacrificed, dreamt, planned.

Ten years jail time, the judge said, but in his unnatural legal jargon. When the constables took his arms on both sides, he knew it was ruthless words. It was words that dehumanize you, that take your freedom away, that doom you to a semi-existence of grey walls, of barbed wire, of rising early and sulk, of jail twilight in your eyes and mind. His address the following ten years: Pretoria Central Jail.

The delivery van passes noisily. This brings him back to the present. He walks down the street. He turns into another street in the direction of the railway station. Maybe there will be a hotel and bar further on. Freedom also means a double whisky or a brandy and Coke or even a tanker of beer. He walks on the pavement in the bright afternoon sunshine and cherishes his freedom. He even becomes excited.

Time for revenge!

He starts getting used to the ordinary.

It is brandy and Coke. The first one he swallowed so that the strong liquor had him gasped at his breath. Toast on his freedom! Now he sits and sips his second, small sips as if he carefully wants to saviour his future, every drop of it on his tongue and in his mind. Like one should carefully taste his liberty.

He also orders a third. He sits and cherishes it, turns the glass around, marvels at the colour, sips as if it is something precious only now and then so that the taste doesn't leave his palate. The plans he contemplated for so many years materialise more concretely, and it makes him restless, but the patience that jail has taught him during eight years keeps his emotions in check.

An hour later, he rises. Freedom also means a few hundred thousand rands if it is still there. A trip by train to Johannesburg is the priority, but then he will have to get a car. Sylvia had a car years ago, maybe presently not, but he cannot involve her now. Hiring a vehicle? No, it would leave a spoor. No parole, no spoor.

"Look, you are an excellent example of someone who can get parole," the parole officer said. "The jails are too full. You have an outstanding record. Clean record. Easily you can get three year respite."

But then you will still look over my shoulder. I must report my address and movements. I must apply when I want to do something outside the parole conditions. Thank you, but no thanks!

"I broke the law. I got a sentence. I will serve my time. It's only fair."

The parole officer just shook his head.

***

The train hastens to Johannesburg. He stares out of the window without noticing the environment. Buildings, areas of grey grass, factories, homes surrounded by neat green gardens, railway stations, platforms with people who scurry to get in or out. It is part of his future life, but he still doesn't feel part of it.

The sun is going down, hastening to creep down to the horizon. It is now a big red ball, tired after the day's work, creeping from behind a few clouds downward. He has a plan with the car.

"Listen, my chum," Jakkie said, "that's no problem. Get to Mayfair station. Then you go to my brother. I'll mention the address only once, maybe here are other ears. Ask for Smiley. Tell him I said he must help you. He is clean. Nothing on his record. He's too clever for the cops." He laughed without a sound as if he hiccups.

Should he get off in Johannesburg and take the tram? He knows he isn't being followed, but it will be nice to vanish in the crowds if he walks from the train station to the tram terminus, only a few blocks away. It will help to while the time.

The city centre at this late in the afternoon is becoming desolate. Like ants, the workers stream to different pickup points, wait in long queues for busses or taxis that engulf them and take them away, each on its own way. There is urgency in the people, impatience to get home, to exchange the long day at work for family, home, food and TV. Especially on Fridays. But he is in no hurry. He stares amazed like a child at the shop windows, the pavement shops, life, freedom! He nearly forgot what he was missing all these years.

The tram to Mayfair is overflowing, and he must stand. However, it is not far. When he disembarks near the station, he asks someone about the street. The man explains hastily and then scurries away. Only a few blocks, take this street.

There is a café on the first corner. He buys a cool drink. He stands and drinks it with his eyes on the entrance and street. Nothing amiss. Outside it quietens. They are in their holes. Together with the late dusk, the people were devoured by the dark.

It is time. He moves out and two blocks from the main road, he finds the street.

62c is painted skew on a piece of board hanging on a dilapidated gate.

"That is not the real entrance, Hannes," Jakkie told him. "Ten yards further on is a gate. But you will have to look carefully. It doesn't look like a gate but as part of the fence. There you will see a hole you will have to put your hand through. Feel to the left. There is a bell. Ring three short ones."

In the dark, he has to look carefully to detect the hole. His hand has difficulty going through but he eventually feels the bell. One, two, three.

He peeps through the hole. In the faint streetlight, he can only make out an uncared space, overgrown with weeds and grass in between the high walls of adjacent buildings. It seems like empty cases, rubbish and empty cans. Jakkie, the fucker, must be laughing his heart out in his cell! Is this a waste of time? But somehow he feels that he is being watched. He shrugs. I shall wait another minute and then I'm gone. Fucking Jakkie! Strange these people of the dusk world of the underworld. He has seen strange people in his eight years in jail.

He turns around to get a hell out, when someone whispers: "Shh, don't talk, Maybe here are other ears."

This sounds familiar. The next moment the gate swings open without a sound and he steps inside. The gate is closed directly behind him. They are in a sort of courtyard. There are more rubbish and debris that he could make out through the hole. A short man walks in front of him on a path through the rubble to an iron gate that looks pinned between two buildings overgrown with ivy. They pass the gate and the midget closes the gate carefully and silently and turns the key to lock it securely. They are now in a small corridor between high walls of probable storerooms.

The little man gestures that he must walk in front. It is dark in this alley. It is an alley where someone can easily plunge his knife to the hilt in your back. His heart beats in his chest and shivers go down his spine.

At the end of the ally, they stop at a wall overgrown with ivy. Baffled Hannes scrutinizes the seemly impenetrable wall. He jumps when the little man sticks his finger in his back. He must step aside and stand still. Then he fidgets between the leaves and knocks three times at the wall and moments later a door opens in front of them. Quickly they step inside.

The door closes behind them immediately.

Instantly they are in another world.

The world of Smiley.

He is watching Karin as she and her dancing partner go through their movements. It is a modern dance with a pulsing rhythm. She executes her movements exquisitely. Her body and the rhythm is one. Her well-built, sexy body in the tight black gown with the daringly low neckline is a beautiful picture under the flashing lights. At this moment, they are dancing apart from each other and their bodies drift back and forth until they suddenly melt tightly into each other's arms.

His whisky leaves a rotten taste in his mouth. With disgust, he sees how the man's hand caresses her bare back, how it lowers to her midriff and then stops at her buttock. He sees when they pass him the undisguised lust on the man's face. He shudders. When they near him again, he gestures to her that he is going to leave.

These parties to which she drags him along, are both predictable and repulsive. Karin on the dance floor seducing the men until one of them glues himself to her and then he leaves. Because Karin will only come home early in the morning as if nothing has happened. She will go into the shower as if she can wash off the flirtations and happily go to the kitchen to prepare breakfast for them. For him and his little son, Stefan.

Slowly he drives in the direction of their home. But first, he must drive to his mother's to pick up little Stefan from her townhouse a few blocks further on. The good lady wanted Stefan to sleep over, but he cannot make peace with it. It is as if he wants to compensate for the infidelity of Stefan's mother. And it is some comfort that he at least tries to keep his family intact. He and Stefan is sort of the main part of the family.

Near the townhouse, his cell phone rings. He answers immediately. Speaks only for a few seconds. He must urgently go to Roodepoort on the West Rand. He glimpses at his watch. It is half-past nine. He should be back before half-past ten. Stefan can stay a little longer at his grandma.

He turns left at the next crossing. His thoughts rush back to Karin. Why does he tolerate it? Why doesn't he divorce her? Why does he allow her to humiliate him? Why does he go along to her Friday parties with the filthy people?

Maybe he still loves her, maybe not. It is probably for Stefan's sake. He is two years of age and innocent. That pair of innocent blue eyes! How will he understand when they are divorced? He simply adores his mother. Then there is also a sort of Calvinistic conservatism in him. Divorce is not part of his vocabulary. He grew up with the idea that divorce is a sin and a disgrace. How will he tell his mother about Karin's escapades?

What is more, how will you tell Karin's parents? Farmers and truly religious people, living a quiet and uncomplicated life on a farm near a small town in the countryside. They have no idea of the intricacies of living in a city like Johannesburg. They are so proud of her and of what she has achieved in her life. A trained secretary with different diplomas, a good marriage, and a beautiful grandson. It is the true fulfilment of their ideals for her. They could give her so little on the salary of a railway worker, but she could escape to an affluent life.

Maybe he tolerates it because he hopes something will happen that change Karin. That she will once again become his bed and marriage mate; that she will get tired of men's sticky attentions, the smell of other men's bodies. That she will long to, like after their marriage, cuddle in his arms.

He sighs and steps on the gas.

Petrus Odendaal, private investigator, one of the best in South Africa. Everyone thinks he is the sun itself and his mates envy him his beautiful, sexy wife.

What a disaster is his life! How do circumstances keep you captured!

***

Smiley is fat, sitting in his expensive chair behind his expensive desk with a thick cigar and keeps his eyes on a monitor. Only when he is completely satisfied that there is no movement outside, he switches it off. The little man moves to the right to a built-in bar. The expensive thick carpet is soft under Hannes' shoes. Between him and the desk stands an upholstered lounge set covered in golden brocade. Big expensive paintings decorate the walls and there are precious marble statuettes on hand-cut wooden tables and a manjefique Chinese vase next to a door opening to the left of the room. To the right is the bar of teak. Amazement shows blatantly on his face.

When he eventually looks at Smiley, he can see on his face that he enjoys the admiration immensely.

It is Smiley who speaks first.

"Wellcome, bra, I'm waiting for you. Jakkie sent a message." He wriggles his corpulent body out of the chair and approaches Hannes with an outstretched hand. Their hands lock in a tight grip. You mustn't underestimate the fat man. He has an iron grip.

"Hello, Smiley, Jakkie is my pal."

Smiley gestures to a chair and they sit down. Smiley sees the curiosity in his eyes.

"You ask nothing and I tell you fuck all. This is my kingdom in the centre of the warehouses. What do you drink?"

"Brandy and Coke."

Smiley's round face lights up. "How's it with Jakkie?"

"More or less fucked up. He sends love and greetings."

"Yes, he will be in for quite a while, the bloody fool. Always too quick to draw a knife. And the rubbish that he knifed wasn't worth anything. And that because of a blooming girl, a whore. But I'm sure you know the story."

He nods. Jakkie told him repeatedly. No one else wanted to listen to the simple story but he listened patiently even if it irritated his ass off. Jakkie has contacts outside, and he didn't want to shut doors.

The little man brings their drinks and makes him scarce in the corner behind the bar counter. They sip their drinks in silence. Hannes knows he shouldn't talk now. This is Smiley's domain and he is calling the shots.

"You say Jakkie is your pal."

Hannes instantly realizes that he can speak his mind now.

"I need a car."

"What for?"

"I must go and fetch something."

"Where?" He shakes his head.

"Not far. I will bring back the car."

Smiley laughs heartily. He holds up one fat hand.

"No, my brother! It doesn't work like this. I sell you a car. It is legal with a license and everything. The cops can't take you. My people know their work. But I never want to see it again. It is yours. It doesn't walk back to Smiley. Cars leave spoors. And these tracks do not walk back to me. If it becomes a problem, drive it into a ditch, leave it next to the road or park it at a station, but I don't want to see it again."

He takes a big swig at his drink and looks intently at Hannes.

Hannes nods. He understands.

"Right. Ten thousand bucks for you." He holds all ten fat fingers in the air. "For someone else it would have been twenty thousand bucks, right?"

"I will have it tonight. I'll bring it."

Smiley smiles as if he wants to say: you have much to learn, although you were in jail.

"You put in in a grocery bag and cover it with veggies and put a 2 litre Coke on top and hand it over to the beggar with the red cap sitting on the corner of the street in front of the station. Through the day is okay. You don't talk to him, just give him the bag and bugger-off. Right?"

"Right."

"Bring another drink," Smiley orders in the direction of the bar.

Again they drink in silence. "Is your story without troubles?"

He watches Hannes carefully.

"If your car is safe, my story is safe." Smiley is satisfied. He leans back and relaxes against the soft cushion. A fat forefinger caresses his fat cheek.

"What else can I do for you? You must tell me now because I don't like visitors all the time."

"That's all for now, except that I need contacts. I won't trample your doorstep."

Smiley laughs loudly. "No, it's okay! But remember, I do passports, IDs, driver's licences, vehicle registrations, girls. Name it, I do it!"

"Jakkie told me you are quite brilliant."

"Ask, my brother, just ask. Even if you want to exchange notes." Again he holds a fat hand in the air. "I know of everything because I have to know of everything."

Thirty minutes later, Hannes has all the contacts he needs. He is impressed.

Smiley smiles from ear to ear. He stands up. "But now I have other business to attend to. Jemima will get you something to eat and take care of you. It is almost seven now. The car should be here by half-past eight. Enjoy yourself. It's free."

He waves at the little man and they vanish through a door behind the desk.

Hannes relaxes and lets his head rest against the cushion. It is heavenly. He closes his eyes. When last did he sit and relax in such luxury? It was last at Sylvia.

"Hello."

He wasn't even aware that the girl entered. She puts down a tray of snacks on a table near him. She is slim and dark with long black hair tumbling over her shoulders. A short red blouse, ring in her navel, short black pants. Very expensive perfume hovers about her.

He wants to get up but she holds up her hand.

"I brought something to eat. Do you want another drink?"

He shakes his head, marvel at her beautiful dark eyes, the full red lips, the smooth, dark skin and the well-formed long legs. She sits down next to him.

"How old are you?" she asks bluntly.

"Thirty-five," he answers baffled.

She laughs. "I am glad. I dislike old men." She shifts up to him and puts her hand on his thigh. Smiles when she feels how he shudders. He peeps around in the room.

"Don't worry. Here is no one. They won't be back before half-past eight."

For a time, he sits motionless. The thought of Sylvia is still in the back of his head, but the exhilaration of this darkhead's touch fires through his body. For a moment, Sylvia is non-existent. Then he looks at the girl next to him. She is willing and waiting for his move. But she is a child. Scarcely seventeen or eighteen. What will Sylvia say when …

"Thanks for the snacks, but you can go. I don't think I am in the mood for …"

She answers lightning quick. "Thanks, it's nice of you."

She is out of the room as quickly as she appeared earlier on.

She can't control her tears. It is a fountain that floods continuously. If she has lost him now for good! The simple sod, why hasn't he let her know? It was better when he was still in jail. She then knew where he was. It was sort of a comfort. Even if he didn't want her to visit him in jail. Eight years. Hell, eight years longing is long, eight years waiting was hell! All she has now is this pain deep in her, heartache and longing, the emptiness of a probable permanent separation. Fucking imbecile!

It was Betsy who read in the newspaper just before closing time of the general amnesty and the inmates that have been released earlier that day. When she arrived at home she phoned the jail. Hannes Van Velden? Released earlier this afternoon.

No address or contact number.

If only she has thought about it earlier. How silly can one be?

Maybe she is even more silly to think that he still loves her. What did he write? Did she interpret it wrongly all these years?

Sylvia

Thanks for your visit. I appreciate it but don't come here again. Also, don't write. It is not fair towards you that I keep you on a string for ten years. You are beautiful and young and if things were normal … But it is impossible now and I want to cut ties with you to give you a chance to carry on with your life. Greetings. Hannes.

She abided by his wish and has never visited him again but each year on his birthday sent him a cake and a card on which she wrote: I'm waiting for you. And she cursed the criminals that caused him to land in jail.

This is the story of my life, she bitterly thinks. Just as I think something falls to my side, life turns its back on me. It was so from her childhood days.

She was raised in poverty. Her father was a real loser that tried with a dilapidated lorry to do transport. Most of the time he had nothing after the lorry broke down and the client refuse to pay the whole amount. She always had, with big sad eyes, to watch her mates buy toffies at the tuck shop, with envy looked at their new school clothes at the beginning of the year, their new shoes, while she had to plod on in last year's rags.

She was clever and in the junior grades she got higher marks than the rest but all the best prizes went to them – the teachers' pets. The only time she felt she was way ahead of them was when the male teacher tried to make sexual advances towards her. It was her last year in primary school and she was already a blossoming beauty somewhat before her time. She smacked him so hard that his goggles shot from his teary eyes and he crawled away like a dog with scabies. That evening she looked at her in the mirror long and searchingly. Why did he try to touch her and not the other, clever, beautiful girls?

The mirror told its own story. Against her wall, she had a portrait of a stunning actress with long, blond hair and a perfect body in a swimsuit. It always was a pleasure to look at her beautiful face and sexy body. Suddenly she saw something of this girl in herself. Long, blond hair, fine face, a developing body. She suddenly realized she had something more than the ordinary rich girls in her class. She decided she should use this new insight and she intensively starts to zoom in on her appearance. No wonder that the son of the doctor asked her to accompany him to the school's final function.

The first few high school years were bliss. Her father got a job as a janitor somewhere. For the first time in her life, there was something extra. They weren't millionaires, but her mother also got a part-time job in a grocery shop. Suddenly there was money for a new dress now and then, for cream for her skin, for makeup. The guys swarmed around about her like bees. She discovered that she could manipulate them with a sway of her hips, while a smile full of promises, with pouting lips, with an unbuttoned blouse that shows promise. She was free of the shackles of poverty that binds you down.

Then life turned his back on them. Her father became a drunk and lost his job. Soon they were poor again. She crawled into a shell, cursed life and hated everyone. She finished school by narrowly scraping through because she had no motivation. In the meantime, Casper tried to be her boyfriend without her encouraging him. He was much older than she was, worked at the mine and had an old car. Because of the car, she didn't chase him away. When she told her mates where they were with the car over the weekends they seemed jealous. And on this envy, how little it might be, she could survive for a week. It cancelled out some of the misery of their poverty.

Casper was a solid guy. Her mother indoctrinated her. "You'll never get another good guy like Casper. Don't let him slip through your fingers." At that stage, the most important thing on earth to her mother was having a husband with a steady job.

When she wasn't able to find a job after school, she married Casper. Her mother was correct. Casper was a solid guy, a good guy. He was faithful to her, loved her, got them a flat. He did extra work because he wanted to buy her a house. She didn't want children before the house was bought. In the meantime, she assisted in a flower shop, mostly administration, but also with flower arrangements. Her little salary also helped and one day Casper took her to a house. It was an old house near the station on a large yard. She was delighted. Casper got a bond and they moved in. She was becoming very fond of him.

He was so proud of her, on his house, on his new car. She organized the house as best she could. She was happy. Her mother was in seventh heaven.

One day she decided it was time for a baby. That evening she would seduce Casper and every evening following until she was pregnant. With anticipation, she waited for him to return from work.

But he would never return. Rockfall deep down in the mine.

Life showed her a backside again. It was like the time when her father became a drunk. The ground beneath her feet gave way. She fell into a deep shaft of depression.

For a year, she lived a meaningless existence. The mine paid out handsomely and helped her to pay off the bond and register the property in her name. At least she had the house but there was not much money to throw around. Betsy at the flower shop simply insisted that she should help in the shop and convinced her to buy a smaller car. It could be used for deliveries and earn her a few bucks.

"It will do you a world of good to get out of the house." Betsy nagged her, but most of the time she loathed the work and wished she could run home and put her head in her pillows and cry. However, it was in the flower shop that her life eventually began to get on course.

He was a long, skinny farmer from the Free State. "Saw my ass," he said. "Lost my farm. Bank took everything. Luckily got a job as a welder. Do you know of any boarding near the railway station? I don't have a car and must use the train. Please, if you know of anything."

They shook their heads. Sorry. Dispirited man. "I've already walked for miles. Will have to look further."

"Sylvia, you have an extra room, don't you? Why don't you take in this poor man?"

She could have kicked Betsy under her ass. She didn't want to be bothered with something like this. She shook her head.

"Listen you can earn a buck or two with this. I'll quickly phone my aunty who takes boarders and hear what she charges."

It was the sudden hope in the man's eyes that softened her heart.

"Maybe temporary; until you get another place."

He moved into her spare room. Then another in the room that would have been the baby's room. And another one in the outbuilding. So, her boarding house took off. The adjustment for her was difficult but the men were decent and because they had to get up very early to catch the train, she was alone in the early morning until she, later on, went to the shop. In the evenings, they were tired and went to their bedrooms early.

Her privacy was a problem with only one bathroom. Also, more rooms, as she frequently had new applications. She counted her money and wondered whether she had enough to build extra rooms. Space on the stand was no problem.

She talked to Betsy about it. Know-all Betsy immediately told her she know of someone. He is busy with alterations in her friend's house and they are very satisfied with his work. She will send a message and the address.

The little man enters the room precisely at half-past nine. Without a word, he gestures. Hannes follows him immediately. They leave the room by exiting through the door behind the desk. Another dark alley. Then they enter some sort of storeroom. Empty boxes, a lot of them. Stacked against the walls and in disorderly heaps throughout the room. Maybe full of drugs and other illegal stuff. The little man leads him through the rubble until they reach a door at the right-hand side. The door leads to an illuminated double garage.

It is a beautiful, white BMW on which its legal owner would have been extremely proud. The little man hands over the keys. He gets in and starts the car but the man gestures he must wait. At a side door, he goes out scrutinizing the vicinity. Then he enters quickly, closes the door behind him and opens the garage door. He indicates that Hannes must go quickly.

Hannes wants to say: say thank you to Smiley, but the little man signifies urgently that he must get the hell out. Moments later, he is in a desolate side street, driving slowly to the main road. He turns left to the west. The car is comfortably hugging him. He knows he must relax, drive within the speed limit so as not to attract attention. Much money awaits him. There is no reason for haunting thoughts. He hid the money well in the old building where he played as a kid for hours. Just for a moment, he has a misgiving. What if the building was demolished? Or it collapsed? Or they had fenced it in? Or someone by flook found the money?

Stop! Relax! You have waited eight years for this. With patience. Even rejected parole. It simply must still be there. Every single note must be there. It is your future. It is the basis of everything you have planned for during the eight years.

And the revenge will be sweet.

He is amazed at how little has changed during eight years. He takes the old main road. He remembers clearly the evening when he came and hid the money. If he was more cunning, he wouldn't be apprehended. He should have known there would be shit when Rothwell suggested they should pool the money; that he knew of safe investments. They should first make sure how much they looted. He can keep it safe and they will split it later on. Hannes only took his bag and got to his truck, and went and hid his money.

Two weeks later, Odendaal took him into custody at Sylvia's boarding house.

He knows the environment. He knows exactly how far to drive, for which beacons he must be on the lookout. This is the environment of his days as a poor kid. He grew up at the little mining hamlet next to the old main road. Phthysis father on mining pension. Ten kids to look after and sometimes other family too. Small overcrowded rooms. Children three on a bed. Always too little food, especially when he was a teenager. Older brothers go to work, leave the house. A little more space. Older sisters leave the house, even more space. Within a year back with a baby. Less space. So, during the day he fled, played for hours around the old mineshaft and the half dilapidated building that probably had been used as a storeroom. He wondered about his future. Factory worker like some of his brothers? Railway workers like some of the others? Conductor? Yes, that is something. Neatly in his uniform. It is the man who controls the train with his sharp whistle. It would be nice to have so much authority. Train driver, perhaps?

Anything to escape this woful existence.

An old chimney in the building with a hole that was plastered shoddily became his secret hiding place. He loosened the bricks one by one and hid his treasure. His paring knife and an old medal he somewhere picked up, and a few loose cents. He packed the bricks one by one back in the opening. It was his treasure. No one would touch it.

In this hole, he hid his part of the loot.

The old bluegum tree is standing on the left-hand side of the road just like eight years before. Gigantic, he is much higher than the trees around him. It is his main beacon. He drives even slower, let faster traffic pass him. Then he stops askew next to the road so that the lights shine on the bushes. Everything is like the past only the bushes are bigger. He knows where the path runs, now overgrown with grass and bushes. He waits until there is no vehicle in sight and drives the BMW quickly in between the bushes.

Branches scratch the car, swing back behind him and make him invisible from the road. He follows a narrow road. The tarmac has crumbled long ago and is bumpy. He can drive very slowly now. No fence. Three hundred meters further the old mineshaft comes into sight. He turns slighty to the right and the old building comes into sight. His heart races. It is still standing. The hole that once contained a door, comforting dark and open.

He stops ten yards from the building and switches off the headlights. The stars and moon make light enough and he would even in the pitch of dark find his way. So familiar and comfortably dark. He climbs out, looks around carefully and goes closer. When he enters the building through the opening, he gets the smell of an old fire. His heart misses a beat. Someone was here. What if … But there is no sound.

He listens intently. Dead quiet. Then he carefully steps into the dark of the room. Only a few yards between him and his money. His heart beats in his chest. His stomach turns.

His hand against the cool wall moves quickly to the dumpy surface, feels with his fingers until he touches it. The bricks stand out slightly. One by one he wriggles them loose and put his hand in the hole. Then he feels it. The flat canvas bag and the thick thread he used to bind the bag tightly to prevent the money from getting wet. He pulls carefully and the bag slithers evenly towards him.

Two arms get him from behind around his body.

"I've got you, you shit!"

5 THE BUILDER

One morning she rose later than usual, somewhat lazy. She wanted to change into her clothes but then remembered Betsy said she had to make arrangements for her kid's sports at the school. She would open the shop later than usual. She would pick up Sylvia for work.

She put on a light summer gown and washed her hair. She was still busy blow-drying her hair when someone knocked on the front door. She was amazed that Betsy had finished all the arrangements so quickly. She shrugged her shoulders. Then there was knocking again. Longer and impatiently.

"I'm coming!" she screamed down the corridor while she tried to bind her hair with a ribbon. Her attempts had the result that her gown fell open and with her hand, she clutched it in front and opened the door for Betsy.

It wasn't Betsy. It was an adonis with dark hair, a square chin, sensual lips, green eyes, with khaki clothes and boots. A man!

"Sorry, I …"

He was out of his depth. She was stunning. The material scarcely hid her full femininity. The gown that fell open, showed well-rounded breasts. She reminded him of the half-naked Greek statues he saw in books on buildings. Wow! She was fantastic!

She was stunned. Just tried to cover her nudity a bit more.

"I am Hannes, the builder."

"Oh, sorry I am like this. I thought it was …"

"Sorry if I'm too early."

"No, you aren't. It is me that is too late. Come in. Sit in the sitting room. I am back in a whiz."

With burning cheeks, she fled and in her room put on a skirt and a blouse.

"I hear you want to add on?"

"I don't know. Depends on the cost."

"How many rooms do you think?"

"I think two. But you must advise me."

"Let me go in and around the house, then we can talk further."

"I'm going to make coffee."

Why is she so jittery? Why does she have a problem getting the cups out of the cupboard?

Later on, finished with their coffee, he asked: "What do you think?"

I think you are wonderful. I think you are the man whose shoes I'd like under my bed. I think those lips of yours are soft and sweet. I think your arms are strong and safe.

Luckily, there was a knock on the door. Betsy let herself in.

Thereafter he visited her frequently. Took measurements, brought temporary plans. They talked it over for hours. She realized that he came because of her. His questions were meaningless. What about ….

Once he joked with her. "Aren't you afraid the men will harass you?"

"No. I'm too expensive. If they hear my prize they never ask again," she jested back. "In any case, the one that gave some trouble had been kicked out by Betsy's boxer brother. I'm not afraid of men. It's nice to have you here!"

Her last comment was not lost on him. His heart beat faster. He also realized that she wanted him to stay longer in the evenings. Talking loosely about the alterations and he must explain about outer and inner walls and can her own bathroom a little bigger. What would be the extra cost? The plans then had already been approved by the municipality.

He could not start immediately. He is on a big project that is a priority.

"I can wait. Until the right time." She glanced at him with meaningful eyes.

Then, one good day, they delivered bricks, cement, sand and gravel. She knew then it was the right time.

That evening he explained. He was on a job that kept him busy until late in the evening, but in the meantime, he will start building early in the mornings at her place. She gave him food and wine.

"Let's drink on the construction," she said. "And come and give me a kiss."

And after they had touched each other, they couldn't get enough of each other. It was more pleasing than in their wildest dreams. In the weeks that followed, he frequently slept over. It was wonderful. She was certain that wedding bells would soon toll. Not that he said anything about it. All that he said was that he wished the other project was completed. She didn't want to push things. You don't push your luck! She intuitively felt that once the project was completed, a new life would begin.

And it had. Only not as they expected.

Eventually, he was finished with her house. She got a private en suite, wisely planned. Another two rooms for boarders that were connected with the other rooms. At last, she had a proper boarding house.

"Today they can finish the painting and clean out the last rubble. Tonight we are going to celebrate." He kissed her exuberantly. She was as exhilarated as a child. She kissed him over and over.

"Leave me for now," he laughed. "I must go to work."

"Work on such a beautiful day? Only BFs do it."

"Then I'm a big one."

Outside the black sedan of Petrus Odendaal stopped. There was a knock on the door. Life changed in an eyewink.

His legs lamely start to shiver under him. Blood drains out of his head. Police! It flashes through his mind. The nauseous feeling on his stomach says it is lost, everything is lost. The arms around his body squeeze tighter. Then the one arm slacks and the next moment he feels the sharp point of a dagger in his back. Sensations flash through his brain. It is like flashing lightning whose might and intensity make you dizzy. Everything futile and in vain!

"You fucker! I'll kill you!"

Then other sensations hit him. The stench of a boozer's breath. The sick smell of a body that hasn't seen water for a long time. The hoarse, unsure voice. Certainly not a case of arrest. Suddenly he knows what is at hand. He also remembers the smell of the burnt-out fire.

With one twitch, he is loose, turning around and pushes the man away from him. The body moves back up to the opening. In the faint light, he sees the bum in his rags.

"Listen," he says quickly, "I won't hurt you. I don't want anything from you. I just came to pick up something that belongs to me."

He holds one arm in front of him to protect him if the bum storms him but the bum's drunk mind works slowly. He is still standing next to the opening.

"This is my place. I sleep here for very long. No one bothers me. What the hell are you doing here? It's my place. It's all I have."

"It's okay. I don't want your place. I just came to fetch something. You can stay here."

He waits for a reaction, but the bum stands still. The excitement of the moment was too much for his foggy mind.

"It is my place," is all he says.

"Listen. Do you want to earn some money? You don't have to do anything."

No answer. "I shall give you money and then I vanish. Then you don't tell anyone I was here, okay?"

Sometimes one's intentions have bad consequences. When the bum hears about money somewhere, he stomps forward. Hannes sees how he comes out of the feint light with a lifted hand with his knife in it. He hits towards where he thinks the man's face would be. Pain shocks through his knuckles when he hits him on the forehead. Without a sound, the bum just collapses. Shock, booze and a mighty blow on his forehead are far too much for him. He lies and squeals like a little pig.

Hannes turns around and grabs his bag. He treads over the crying body hastening to the door opening. He takes out a note and throws it at the bum. Then he flies to the BMW. Minutes later he is on the main road approaching a suburb of Johannesburg.

It is far more than he anticipated. In his hotel room he counts the beautiful R200 and R100 notes one by one. Almost R500 000. And then there are golden Kruger coins of which he can't guess the value. The lot of money makes him dizzy but he also now calculates how much the other guys would have pocketed. Six bags they looted and he took the smallest one and went off. But it is senseless to worry about that now. To his plans, it will make no difference should he know.

Firstly, he considers driving to Sylvia. However, he decides against it. The day was too hectic, his nerves are too shattered, the exhilaration about the money too great. He packs everything in a new, neat little suitcase, locks it and locks it in a cupboard. The key he buries under his pillow. Then he orders a bottle of whisky. A few tots and then a long night's rest. In any case, it is almost eleven-o'-clock.

He sleeps that night like a satisfied millionaire.

Waking up is like the blessing of rain over the dusty city. Refreshing! Through his window, he watches the silver streams from heaven, faintly hears the rumble of the morning traffic, sees how the clouds make way for the sun's rays. Clear and brilliant! Birds fly freely past his window, frantic after the early shower. This is the first time in eight years he has awakened free and out of jail. In the distance, the thunder slowly subsides.

A new, clear, clean-washed day, a day for planning, a day for the future.

He orders a hefty breakfast from room service. Everything he had to forfeit in jail. Bacon, eggs, yoghurt, beef sausages, cheese, toasted bread, marmalade, and coffee. Who is this super-rich guy in South Africa? Oppenheimer. This morning he feels like an Oppenheimer. He can pay for everything his heart desires.

Ten-o'-clock he leaves the hotel. A busy day lies ahead. Even now, he can't decide. Should he go to Sylvia? When will he go to Sylvia? She is still waiting for him. She wrote in her last letter two months ago with his birthday. She will wait patiently for another two years.

But first things first. He drives towards the city, gives the package to the bum on the corner without a word. Then he starts with his shopping. It leads him to weird places in unsavoury suburbs. He must wait for hours because of security reasons before he gets what he wants and he has to pay heavily for the stuff. Sometimes he must wait for the goods to be fetched from another place. But he is satisfied. Jakkie and Smiley's names open doors for him literally and figuratively. Especially when they ask him if he knows Smiley. If so, things are handled much quicker. Many of these contacts are ex-inmates. This is the Johannesburg underworld. What you need is available at a price.

The jail in itself is an education on its own. A strange population, street skunks, knifers, burglars, murderers, fraudsters are thrown together from different outside worlds. For him, the most interesting blokes were the doctors, attorneys, senior clerks, and brokers. Most of them swindling money out of others' pockets into their own. Chaps who with open eyes cheated people. In them, he saw Van Zyl, Schoonraad, Rhoode, and Rothwell. The guys that dug his grave.

They have no conscience. As one broker told him: "I could have been a multimillionaire. Things only got a little wrong."

"What about the people who lost thousands because of your schemes?"

"Oh, tough luck for them. If the Oriental flu didn't creep into the money markets, I could have made thousands upon thousands for me and them."

Hannes only shook his head. If someone must go and sit in jail for you for ten years so that you can make millions, it doesn't bother you.

But he learned from them.

So damning as their betrayal of him, so damning will be the revenge he is going to inflict on them. One by one. That he swore in the court the day he was sentenced. He had discussed it with Jakkie many times. Jakkie knows how to kill people.

But Jakkie was only a street thug, not a sophisticated killer. It was his fifth year in jail when Gaffels arrived. He was a long, unkempt dude with big eyes and a long donkey face. Not the sort of man Hannes would like to call a friend.

"Caught a guy with my wife in bed. I shot him to hell. He thought I was still at the bar when I returned home. That whore I chased naked down the road. Shot at her but missed. Life sentence, your honour. Fuck you! I kept my trap shut and say sweet all! Must maybe be my home." He waved his arm.

Gaffels had a big mouth. It was his stories that incited Hannes.

"Listen here, my chum. A blaster like me you will not get very easily. Those layers of coal can sit where they want. When the shift boss said: 'Gaffels, get them out', I just sat there and look at the layers, and I watched them, those coal in their layers. And I said: 'Don't you worry boss.' And then my head began to spin as I calculate everything. Blasting, my mate, is an art. The guy that drills holes randomly and ignites the dynamite sticks only makes a fuckup. Not me, I watch them and when my head has spun enough, I say: drill here, drill there, put in so many sticks here and so many there. And when we are finished and the fuses ran … Bang! There the coal lies in a nice heap, neatly extracted, and I don't talk shit."

Some just threw their heads back and laughed. The others just shook their heads. In the jail, you hear many shit stories.

Hannes went and sat down next to Gaffels. "I want to learn everything about blasting."

Gaffels closed his one eye and draw on his cigarette.

"To do what?"

"This has bugger-all to do with you."

"Okay! You want to learn everything about blasting."

"Everything you know. I will pay you as well."

"Right. You are with the best man. The king of blasting in Africa."

He absorbed. Explosives, fuses, triggers, charges; everything Gaffels could tell him. Every day something new. He asked to be transferred to the library from the building section. There he could order books about explosives and explosions; over the newest controlled technology. He ordered a massive amount of information. He studied it meticulously. It was fascinating. You could think an explosion is only an explosion but bomb letters, land mines, and hundreds of others are fascinating different but also the same.

And the electronics! Remote bombs, time bombs, land mines. In time, he specialised in remote bombing. It was fascinating. A time switch is good and well, but the moment you have switched it on you lose control. The thing runs on its own. Remote is more direct, the moment of action and the explosion coincide.

He was amazed at the paring of the wires. It seems to him like the veins that run through your body and eventually come together at your heart. Wires that leads the current to the contact points. He could see everything like a diagram before him. The signal from the remote, the activation of a magnet, the contact between two points and boom! The day he left the jail, he was one of the most educated persons on bombs in South Africa.

"Smiley," Jakkie told him, "Smiley can tell you where you will get the goods. He had made many of the things in '76. The boys paid and Smiley smiled." He laughed without a sound at his own joke.

Late that afternoon he is satisfied that he has obtained everything necessary for his plans. Leisurely he drives to one of Smiley's contacts and hides his loot there. In a desolate warehouse, he locks his bag with the loot in a safe, stuff the key deep into his pocket and drives in the direction of the central business district.

What he put in the back of his mind the whole day, now becomes a compelling reality. The choice: to Sylvia or not? He stops at a bar. More than an hour later, he is still sitting there. He can't make a final decision. He orders another drink. Thinks.

One day he was fed-up with the overfull cramped home. A builder, who was erecting a few more houses for the mine, was building nearby. Frequently he loitered around there. It was fascinating to see how skilfully the old man get the mortar on his trowel and neatly deposit it on the bricks.

How he then put the brick neatly in place and scratches the surplus mortar off neatly amongst the building line.

Neatly, row upon row. Sometimes he passed bricks to the old man or packed them on the scaffold. The old man talked to him, mostly about building, about guys that crooked him, about the mortar that falls from the walls overnight if it is too cold.

On that day he walked to the old man.

"Uncle, I'm looking for a job."

The old man didn't answer him, just continued packing bricks on the wall.

"I want to work for you. I want to become a builder."

"It is hard work."

"I don't mind. I shall work hard." He knew that if the uncle didn't give him a job he would in any case leave his home. He was more than fed-up. The sad thing was that he could not blame anyone. The situation has just become intolerable. He simply had to escape from it.

The old guy stopped working and with the back of his left hand swept over his sweated forehead.

"What about school? You young people must become learned."

"I can't learn at home." He wanted to add somewhat but the old guy just shook his head.

"Your parents?"

"They can't choose for me, Uncle. They have too many others over which they must decide." And too many mouths to feed, he wanted to add.

"How far are you at school?"

"I've got Grade 10. I can leave school now."

He waited in anticipation.

"I need hands, that's true ... hand over those bricks ... but I don't know, I can't pay much. I'm only subcontracting and I will have to train you. And you are going to shit, my boy, building is hard work."

"I don't mind, Uncle. I shall work hard, you'll see." The old man only laughed.

"And where are you going to stay?"

"I shall sleep at the back of your truck." The old man laughed heartily.

"I've got a small outbuilding where you can stay. But it's empty. At first, you'll have to sleep on the floor. The auntie will give you food, but I say again. I can pay you next to nothing."

"It is okay, Uncle. You will see …"

"Go and speak to your parents. I depart at five-o'-clock."

He was back long before five. There was nothing to talk about. He only said he got a job and he was leaving. He will visit them once in a while. His mother gave him two old blankets. He put all his rags in a shopping bag and walked off. He couldn't really think or feel. It was something that must be done. You don't think about it.

He really suffered during the night in the extreme cold under the paper-thin blankets on the concrete floor. Later on, he got cardboard and put it down like a mattress. It helped a bit. And his painful body! His back constantly hurt, his hands with blister upon blister eventually turned to calluses. Sometimes he felt like crying from the intolerable pain. The auntie gave him some ointment when she saw how scabby and injured his hands were. And the food! Always too little for a young, growing, hardworking boy.

But he worked. There was no choice. This or bugger-all. First, he had together with the handyman, mix concrete or mortar. Hours upon a day. Some days there was a weariness in his body. Then the handyman joked.

"It seems to me you've got porridge in those muscles of yours. You white guys can't do any work. Don't wrestle with the spade. Work like a machine. Oh my, you have much to learn!"

When they stop in the afternoon and he exhaustedly lean against the truck, the strong, fit Zulu jested with him.

"You must go to bed early tonight. Tomorrow we are going to throw the foundation. You are going to shit, my boy!"

But slowly his muscles developed. His young, lanky body changed into a muscled, lean body and his spirit became tough, and every evening he had more energy left, and he learned to pack bricks faster than his boss. After two years it was he who chided.

"Come, my Zulu friend. Maybe you have eaten too much this morning. Or are your cannabis finished? You must go to bed early. Tomorrow will be a rough day."

The Zulu laughed with white teeth. "The chicken has become a cock."

He still resided in the small room. His wage remained the same because the auntie wanted him to pay for the boarding. He didn't care. It was valuable training. He was quite satisfied with his arm and breast muscles, with his stamina, with the precision he could lay bricks. And he learned.

How to read plans, to put out foundations, the construction of different kinds of roofs. He wanted to know everything.

The old man one day said: "I can't teach you anything more."

He looked pensively over the field knowing that his building days are almost done. He knew the young man can go much further than he ever came. And he can't prevent him from resigning.

But Hannes' loyalty towards the old man was unwavering. He thought with great love and thankfulness of the chance the old man gave him in life. Although he had very few earthly possessions, he had knowledge and expertise. In his simplicity, he compared himself with his schoolmates. Sometimes he saw them in the CBD. Aimless loiterers, out of work or left work, some using drugs and steal for a living. Although he struggled immensely, he didn't turn out a crook. Every month he took a few cents home. Then they all said how proud they are of him for working so steadily.

He wouldn't drop the old man because there was Rachel as well.

Rachel and her father and mother moved into the home next door one night. When he washed at the tap the next morning, she stood and stared at him from the fence a metre from him, her jersey pulled tightly around her. Alone and vulnerable. He felt uneasy without a shirt and simple PT trousers. The trousers was his sleeping gear.

"Good morning," he simply said, "did you move in last night?" She was about the same age as him. She didn't answer, just shook her head and the long, brown hair made waves and she looked at him with big, brown eyes.

"My name is Hannes," he tried clumsily to get a conversation going. She only stared at him and he even felt more uneasy.

"You are marvellous," she suddenly said, turned around and fled into the house.

During the next few weeks, he couldn't help himself thinking about her. She was a beautiful girl, even if he only got a glimpse of her once in a while. Strange woman, he thought. But suddenly he couldn't work the urgent desires out of his body and thoughts. A few weeks later she again stood next to the fence.

"Hello ..."

"Rachel."

"Hello, Rachel."

"Hello, Hannes."

They started talking. She wanted to know why he lodged outside and not with his parents.

He laughed: "They are not my parents. The old man is my boss." He told her of his past. She stared at him with her big, brown eyes. He then wanted to know about them.

Her father is dead. This man is her stepdad. He works in a factory but gambles himself so frequently into a tight spot that they had to move overnight to prevent his creditors catching up to him. That is how they ended up here. Until one of them found out their new place and then they would move overnight again. But not for long. She is busy with a diploma at the Technical College as secretary and typist and the course was almost completed. As soon as she had work, it would be goodbye.

"I want to see your place." She walked along the fence and found a place she could climb over. He wanted to object, but she was over already.

Reluctantly he led her to his room. He was self-conscious that his clothes were strewn all over, that his bed was unmade, that he had neglected to clean the place properly. Her eyes swept over his sparse belongings, the lopsided cupboard against the wall, the iron bed with the coconut hair mattress, the table on which a magazine and a few books on building techniques were that he bought in a second-hand shop, a dilapidated old armchair, a washing table with a bowl and a cracked mirror against the wall.

She was ecstatic.

"All this is yours?" He nodded. "I wish I could also stay alone."

He didn't understand then. Only later, he realized that she too tried to break with a shoddy past and suffocating circumstances. His poor room for her was a palace, a place where you are the boss, where you are not compelled by silly rules like not taking a too-long bath, where you were not scolded by a grumpy stepdad. Where you could be free!

She watched herself in the mirror, swiped over her frock, pushed her hair in position.

"There isn't even such a big mirror in our home. This is wonderful."

From then on, she climbed over the fence frequently. They became friends. They could talk for hours over their ideals, gave advice to each other as best they could. They agreed on one thing: life is no joke. Outside there are a lot of fuckers you can hate without remorse.

It was a hot Saturday afternoon. He had to fasten a corrugated roof in the bloody sun the whole morning. The uncle and auntie were away to their children He lied on his bed for a while, but it was too hot. A thunderstorm was developing and it was stuffy. He took off his clothes, put on his white PT shorts and went to the tap outside. He felt dirty.

She was suddenly at the fence. Shorts and a loose blouse. "Do you want to bathe?"

Question marks in his eyes.

She laughed. "My people are away for the weekend. There is no one at home. What about a nice bath?"

This was an attractive proposition. When last had he bathed properly?

"Everything is there. Just bring your towel. I'm going to fill the bath."

He fetched his towel. She was preparing the bath for him. It was the smell that hit him. It reminded him of his mother and sisters' bath soap at home. The smell here was overwhelming. She turned the taps down when the bath was half. She took a bottle, turned off the lid and poured some of the creamy ingredients into the bath. She stirred the water. He was amazed to see how a layer of foam formed on the surface.

"Okay, get in."

Shyly he indicated that she must go. She laughed and went out. So much luxury he hasn't experienced in his whole life. The warm water and foam pleasantly surrounded him. He succumbed to the luxury of foam and scented soap.

"I shall wash your back." She was back suddenly. "Your hair also if you wish."

He allowed her to caress his head and back. She left. He was finished and pulled on his shorts. This was a wonderful experience. She waited for him outside the door. He tenderly took her in his arms.

"No, not here. Let's go to your room. I want to tell you something."

He had difficulty containing his passion. In his room, she sat down on his bed. He sat down next to her.

"My mother and stepdad went to a town in the south."

"You told me."

"Do you know what it means?"

"No."

"We must move again."

She was silent for a moment.

"He must run away again. I heard when they were talking. He is going to ask for lodging at his brother's smallholding near Vereeniging."

"And you?"

"I will have to go with. What else? Luckily, the classes of the course are finished. I just must take the exam if there is money for a train ticket."

"I will lend it to you."

Her big, brown eyes were full of tears. "Thanks, I will pay it back as soon as I've got work."

"It doesn't matter. You are not going to let the fuckers win."

"I won't. And I am going to long for you." She stroked his back and shivers ran through him.

"I am going to long for you too." He put his arm around her. She cuddles close to him.

"Now I want to kiss you."

They surrendered to the passion they carried in their bodies.

After the weekend, they were gone. Probably he wouldn't see her again. About the money, he wasn't stressed. It was more than money's worth.

After the old man one day fell from the scaffold, he knew it was the end of an era. The old man died soon afterwards and the auntie moved in with one of her children somewhere. He considered going on his own but decided against it. He was too young to be an independent building contractor and he knew too little of the administration. He got a job at a big, building company.

It was like manna from heaven. A healthy salary, compared to his previous wage. He distinguished himself as a hard worker, could move to a reasonable room in a boarding house, had enough to eat and, above all, had opportunities. That he took with both hands. With the architects and quantity surveyors, he studied plans, learned modern building techniques, which concrete mixtures used for different pillars and floors and of reinforced concrete. In time, he was given more responsibilities to order equipment and building materials. It was heaven on earth.

Janitor meant a free cab. A salary double his. It meant helping with the planning, preliminary investigation of sites together with the architect and the developers. That was what he wanted and knew he was qualified after five years at the company.

This was the post becoming available. He applied.

"It will be only a formality," the staff officer assured him. "No one is more qualified for the job than you are."

Then the shock. The architect was furious.

"You should have been appointed. Now I must work with that little shit … I really don't know what the guys on top think, but if you are the son in law of one of the directors …"

It was a bitter pill to swallow. After he and the shit of a janitor had some disagreement, he thought of leaving the company to start his own contracting business. It was not so difficult to decide after he met Rachel by chance in Johannesburg. They were busy with a shop in the CBD. Lunchtime he went to a restaurant to have something. Scarcely had he sat down when the brown-eyed girl entered and looked around for an empty seat. He waved at her and she came and sat at his table.

"Goodness, Rachel, you look marvellous." It wasn't the Rachel from next door anymore. This was a sophisticated, well-dressed lady, beautiful in a blue skirt and white blouse on high heels, self-assured and well-cared for.

She smiled pleased. "You look not so bad either."

She worked at a big business. Yes, she got her diploma and a good job. But she aimed at higher things. She also took courses in office administration and luck was with her. A brilliant job as the boss's private secretary. She is happy.

"And the other gender?" He suddenly thought back to his room.

"Oh, that. The boss's son. I target him and they are filthy rich. Do you know, even if I work for a boss, I feel free. I do my own thing. By the way, I owe you money."

He laughed heartily. "It was a greater pleasure than you can think of. Maybe I owe you more than you owe me."

So, she's doing her own thing. Maybe it's time for me to do the same. Things won't come right at the job anymore.

"You must make sure you will survive. The building profession is tough." The architect was really sorry that he decided to leave.

He resigned and was amazed at how well it went. Until Rothwell came on the scene. Not long after that Odendaal took him in custody at Sylvia's place.

Sylvia? It is a difficult decision.

It is well past nine when he drives west. In the end, he knew it would be like this. He just cannot stay away. At about ten he knocks on the door. Expectation and anxiety wash over him. Shouldn't he rather have stayed away? The door opens.

She stands there with the bright light of the sitting room behind her. Blond hair like a waterfall over her shoulders. Sleeping gown tightly around her.

"I thought it was Betsy," she whispers amazed. It seems as if something is wrong with her focus. He stands wavering. What now?

"Hello, Sylvia."

"Hannes!!" She literally flies towards him, hugs him tightly and then starts to cry shamelessly. "Hannes," she whispers again and then starts to kiss him exuberantly, his lips, his cheeks, then she kisses him full on the mouth. His arms encircle her, hug her softly against him and then more tightly.

"Sylvia." He can scarcely pronounce her name. Hell, he longed for this girl and she is so glad that I am here, flashes through his brain. Suddenly he feels as if he has come home.

"I thought …"

"I shall tell you everything later on. The prez gave some of us off. It is nice to be here with you."

She drags him by the hand through the sitting room. In her room, only a bedlamp makes a faint light. She closes the door behind them.

"I've waited so long for this," she whispers almost inaudible.

The boarding house is empty this weekend. All the tenants are gone to their families. For a few days, they are alone. Only he and she and their love and passion.

"I thought I would have waited for another two years. You shit, why haven't you let me know?"

"I could have been out long ago. But I wouldn't. I would like you to yearn for me a little longer. But the prez said the jails are too full. Take your things and bugger-off. We are now tired of your trap," he jokes.

"How someone can get tired of your face … Come give me a kiss." Then she cuddles in his arms, kisses him all over, ruffles his hair. He hugs her warm body tightly, surrender to her caresses, shivers when she strokes him lightly. Three days of bliss, three days of making up for the time they've lost.

Somehow, they both know they have to talk. The present will soon become the future and how you wish to preserve moments of happiness, they also pass. Tomorrow and the days thereafter is a future for which you must plan and what you plan now, has consequences for what you are going to decide tomorrow. You never escape the future, the present or the past.

"And now?" she asks on Monday evening.

He doesn't answer.

She remains quiet. His last words in court still spook her. She felt like him. The contemptible skunks! How could they do it to him! They were even more blameworthy than he was. How could they do it to her? Especially Rothwell, the low, cunning snake. But now with him at her place? What now?

He mustn't leave. He simply must not!

10 SCHOONRAAD

Willem Schoonraad is quite happy. He had a good night's rest. It is Friday and the weekend winks. His holiday home at Jeffreys Bay is waiting. He must deter himself not to jump in the car and race to the sea. Maybe, Sonia, his secretary, is there already, his wife in Johannesburg.

He smiles when he enters the lounge and fills a glass with orange juice. He looks around. The place is almost full. On one side, a bearded man sits at a table alone. At a bigger table, sit a few teenage girls giggling. No, that's not what he fathoms. He walks over to the table of the bearded man.

"Sorry, Sir. The tables are full. Do you mind me sitting with you?"

"With pleasure. Please sit down. I'm alone."

"Thanks, my surname is Schoonraad. Sorry …"

"No problem. I'm Wolmarans. No problem. I'm going to get some fish …" Hannes has great difficulty keeping calm.

Eating their eggs, bacon and toast they talk, or rather Schoonraad talks. He likes to brag about his successes. He is part of the development of a golf country club.

"Wow! For that you need a lot of money, not so? It is totally out of my league. I'm only a builder who came to investigate some prospects here. What is the cost of such a project?"

"Oh, it cost an arm and a leg." Schoonraad is in his element, leans forward as if he wants to divulge a big secret. "You see, the secret is to get guys with money to develop the country club. If you get enough fish, you need not invest millions. And there are a lot of guys that now want to come aboard, and then you pocket."

He sat up straight with a big smile on his face.

"I see, but you have to have something?"

"Yes, you must, but you also must be clever. Let other guys' money work for you. Listen, about eight years ago I struck some luck." He grins while he rinses the last of his coffee through his mouth as if he is giving away a big secret. "I bought the land, you see. This has been vacant for eight years. Recently, I began to advertise to get guys who are interested in this sort of thing. And that's it! Listen, I must go. Quickly go and have a look that no one befuddles me."

He winks at Hannes, puts down his cup and stands up. "Here is my business card. If you are interested in this sort of investment, contact me."

Suddenly he hesitates. "Haven't we met before somewhere?"

For a moment there is a piece of ice in Hannes's stomach but he forces himself to answer as evenly as possible.

"I don't think so."

"Come have a look at the golf course, it is something to see."

"I will see if I have time, mister Schoonraad, thanks in any case."

You low pig, Hannes surmises when Schoonraad has left. While I sit in jail, your stolen money is safely invested in property. While my money is divulged by inflation, yours are growing like the grass on that piece of land. And because you have it, you can entice investors to pay dearly for parts of the land. The resentment he has felt all these years in jail is now a burning fire. You must be clever, you said. Maybe your shrewdness will become your downfall.

Later on, he drives out to the development. He is amazed by the massive machinery that devours pieces of land and spits it out on another place. So can man fuckup nature. A hillock was demolished to make way for a clubhouse. The golf course is entrapped in man's power. Beautiful, powerless, green hillocks exchanged for patches of green and ribs of grass. Sprayers spitting life on the grass, sandpits like skeleton bones white in the sun.

He goes and sits in his car. They ravage everything. Like the hillock and nature must be used, also the instruments for their purposes have to be used like him years ago. It is not you that determine your future. It is the wealthy, the powerful, the money wolves, the unscrupulous. Money is their god, man's greed the upper-god. He has difficulty with the bitterness in his mouth and in his heart.

He starts the car. He has a very important appointment.

***

Schoonraad says goodbye to the contractors. It is four-o'-clock. Now for Jeffreys. Just past Knysna he puts on his flicker and turns right. He has to fill up his car. He listens to the radio and the weather report. Beautiful sunshine is expected for the whole weekend. Good. An exhilarating weekend awaits him. When he drives out, he had to wait for a black cab also wanting to fill up. He peeps at the driver. A darkish, young man with a ponytail. He laughs. It takes all sorts to make the world.

Schoonraad drives fast but within the speed limit. A sort of weekend tranquillity creeps over him. Deep down there is the exhilaration of relaxing, yachting, swimming and then of course the sexy Sonia. He smiles happily and looks in the mirror. Far behind him comes the black cab keeping almost the same speed. The distance remains almost the same, although the cab seems to come nearer.

***

The lady's voice is sweet. She sings her usual rhyme.

"Lady," the voice says through a handkerchief, "this is Willemse from Mister Schoonraad's place on Jeffreys. I can't get hold of him on his cellphone. There is a fire in his house. Can you try …"

"Oh no, Sir. I'll phone him immediately …"

The cell phone is killed even before she has completed her sentence. This will put ants in Schoonraad's trousers, he thinks. He climbs out of the car and throws the cellphone over the abyss. Maybe someone will one day pick it up. He makes sure that the bump in the road over which Schoonraad must drive, is clearly in his vision.

Schoonraad's cellphone rings.

This is the receptionist in his office in Johannesburg.

"Sir," she sounds alarmed, "Willemse from your house in Jeffreys has just reported a fire in your house. He wants to know where you are …"

Dammit! Must it be happening now? He looks in the mirror. The black cab is fifty yards behind him. His serenity is gone. He floors the gas pedal.

***

The green Mercedes comes over the bump sooner than he has expected. And even more speedily. He smiles and strokes habitually over his left cheek. He feels the scar under his beard from a knife in the jail. It was meant for his throat he knows, but he could dodge it and he also knows it was Rothwell and his scaly buddies who organized it. His finger remains on the red button. Payday.

For a moment, he wishes he could have heard the conversation between Schoonraad and his massively upset receptionist but now he must focus on the green Mercedes racing down the road. Through his binoculars, he can see how Schoonraad fidgets with his cellphone. His finger presses the red button slightly.

In the days after the first day in court, while he was out on bail, she heard the full story. One day Rothwell came to him on a building site. He wanted an office complex built. He has the plans. Would Hannes have a look and work out a quote? He also will get other quotations. The terrain is a bit rough, but they had it levelled with a bulldozer. To make sure they have no problem with the rock layer near the hill, they had already dug a few test holes. The ground is gravelly, but there aren't rocks. Can he get the quotation within a week at his office in Johannesburg CBD?

Hannes had a look and found everything exactly as Rothwell had described it. He also checked the test holes. Yes, the rest of the terrain was gravelly and somewhat impacted by heavy machinery, but nowhere rocks surfaced. He worked out a quotation and delivered it to the luxurious office at the secretary. A week later Rothwell phoned him for an appointment.

"Congratulations. It is a brilliant quotation. I accept. It is not much cheaper than the others, see, but I checked your history and I'm sure I've got the right man." The habit of Rothwell to see everything irritated him later on to no end.

With him was another man. Rhoode, his attorney.

"I've asked Dave to draw up a contract in the meantime, see. He is my right hand. He will handle the rest of the things. When can you start? It is quite urgent, see."

"I'll start next week with the foundations. I need a week to finish up my current project."

"Marvellous, good! We can leave the dates as in the contract, Dave. There will be ample time to finish this project and remember, don't worry too much about the penalty clause. I rather want a sturdy building."

He and Dave glimpsed at each other and smiled. Then already they had him in their pockets. He only realized that afterwards.

"Now you must excuse me. I've got another appointment. You and Dave can sort out the rest."

Dave pulled a hefty contract nearer when he had left.

"Okay, it is just the normal thing. You can take time and read it through. Some parts are quite technical with a lot of Latin words, so I suggest we go through it quickly while I explain everything. I will give you a summary of the whole thing then we finish quickly. The first part …"

He talked quickly. Today Hannes knows it was a lot of trash, but then he was young and inexperienced and didn't want to look stupid. With his quick tongue, Rhoode watched Hannes carefully. When he saw something was unclear to Hannes, he assured him it was not crucial, except if one of them broke the contract deliberately, and that wouldn't happen, would it? The contract was intended to safeguard both parties.

"By the way …" he delved in his briefcase and got a cheque out. Mister Rothwell insisted that I give you an advance. The thing is quite important to him."

Hannes signed the contract. Satisfied Rhoode stuffed it in his briefcase, invited him for a beer that he declined, and they left the office on the sixth floor and went to the lifts.

Monday morning he left three workers behind after he had measured out the foundations. They had to begin with digging out the foundations. When he arrived late in the afternoon, they had done sweet all.

Rocks, they explained. They can't grow. At some places, it was hard rock about 200 mm under the gravel, in other places even less. Where they had to grow deeper at the incline, it was rock all the way.

He let the workers remove the loose soil. The test holes were dug neatly at places where no foundations were necessary. In between the rocks, the bulldozer skilfully dumped soil over the rocks and compacted it. He phoned Rockwell immediately.

"Mister Rothwell is overseas for three weeks. Can I take a message for him?"

What now?

Pneumatic drills were the only answer. At the tempo they could bore through the rocks and make foundation furrows, he estimated that he would meet the deadline with difficulty. He pacifies himself that Rothwell had said that he shouldn't worry too much about the penalty clauses, but he felt the thing was slipping.

However, a few weeks later he estimated if things run smoothly from then on, he could deliver on time or just a little late. Full of hope he drove to the building site on Monday morning, just to be shocked out of his boots. There was almost nothing! The workers and the corrugated store in which they slept, the storeroom with doorframes, window frames and all his equipment were gone. Only a heap of sand and piles of bricks remained. It was a clean sweep.

He tried again to contact Rothwell but he was on a hunting trip.

He had to delve even deeper in his cash to replace everything and hire new workers. He felt life was turning its back on him. They had to work extra shifts that cost him. He was desperate to get reliable workers, he hated rainy days, he got up the scaffolds and worked the blood out of his fingers. Somewhere deep in him, he got the feeling that there was a total onslaught against him? Why the rocks? Why the stealing? Why when he asks Rhoode for a payment, he gets a cold shoulder? Something was amiss!

On a nice Friday morning, a courier brought a letter from Rhoodie to him. Because he is behind schedule the first penalty clause now come into operation. A lot of ununderstandable legal gibberish of which he could only make out that the case would be contested in court. Any payment that might come due would be suspended and a penalty amount per day was now payable to Rothwell.

He tried to phone Rothwell. The receptionist was over-friendly and he knew she lied. He is not available and every query should be directed to Rhoode's office. A few days later another letter. He had to finish the building on the schedule laid out in the contract to prohibit serious legal consequences. He should remember to pay the penalty fees or else they would be forced to remove him from the site and confiscate all his equipment.

He was fucked! He couldn't go ahead. He couldn't pay penalization, he couldn't get out of this situation.

One day Rothwell phoned him. Can he visit the office so that they can fix the problem?

"I think this project is not worth our friendship. I will get someone else to finish, don't worry. I need you for something else, see. He waved at the contract. It was only a case of a confluence of circumstances." Later he would know that Rothwell planned everything meticulously, even before he handed in his quotation and he signed his demise.

Rothwell wanted Hannes to build a shop at the back of the bank that he wanted to rent out. He shouldn't worry about Rhoode's letters. He didn't handle the case with tact as he should have. From now on Rothwell himself would take care of Hannes. Here was another advance.

Hannes was uneasy but financially he was so bankrupt that he could not resist. And he started at Sylvia and wouldn't take a cent from her for now.

He built. Money was deposited regularly in his account. It was only the outer walls and a roof he should build. That's all Rothwell wanted for now. Small windows in front. They should cover them up. They were nearly finished with the plasterwork when Rothwell late in the afternoon pitched up with a gas lamp and a bottle of expensive whiskey.

"Let your workers go. We are going to celebrate." Then the game began. They sat down at the back wall next to a table with the plans on it.

Rothwell was very jovial. Told Hannes about his ventures, his overseas, and hunting trips.

He could see Hannes is waiting for an explanation. "Look, I still have a hold on you. I can activate those penalty clauses at any time." He laughed and patted Hannes lightly on the arm. "But I am not such a man. Don't want one of my mates in trouble. And we are mates, aren't we?"

Hannes was a little relaxed and slightly intoxicated. Maybe the issues at the shop complex were silly unpredicted events. Maybe Rothwell wasn't so bad at all. But he was still uneasy. He suspected that Rothwell was not playing open cards with him. His tongue was too slick and the friendliness plastered on too thick.

After another drink, Rothwell played his ace.

"Why do you think I am building here?"

"No idea." Rothwell laughed out loudly.

"The bank, see."

"The bank?"

Rothwell took a great swig. "The bank, the safe, see." Hy bumped his finger against the wall. Hannes didn't understand.

"We are sitting only half a metre from millions, see."

"It is the bank's."

"It can become ours, see." He poured another drink. Hannes felt cold shivers running down his spine.

"You mean …?"

"That's right. This is where you come in, see."

"Me?"

Rothwell stayed quiet for a while allowing Hannes to let his words sink in. Then he took a plan out of his pocket. It was a plan of the bank. A simple drawing with the safe indeed only a half metre from them. Only two walls between them and hundreds of thousands. The one Hannes built and then probably a reinforced wall of the bank.

Hannes was flabbergasted. "But how do you …?"

"Not me. You!" Rothwell took out cigarettes. Hannes took one absentmindedly. "You are the main ingredient of the plan, see, else …"

The plan was worked out in detail He should work from then on in the afternoons and during the evenings when the bank was closed. Earlier in the evenings, there are some movement in the streets but later it was quiet. He shouldn't make haste but work leisurely and alone. A hole through which a man can climb with a bag full of money was all that was necessary. But he must go slowly about this. Go through the first wall and then slowly calf away the next wall and go through the reinforcement so that only a thin layer on the inside of the bank remains. When he was so far, they will on a Saturday night, after he had taken leave for a week or two, break through that layer. Their alibi would be that someone burgled the bank. They were simply not there.

Hannes' lips were dry; his intestines knotted. "The security system?"

"Inside information. It was installed so that it focuses on the door of the safe. But we are coming from the back end. The alarm wouldn't go off. They will discover it only on Monday, see."

"And say someone get a sniff in the nose?"

"It is your job to make sure. Inside the bank, I will take the responsibility."

Hannes was so overwhelmed that he swallowed the whole glass of whisky in one shot.

"And if I …"

Rothwell smiled broadly. "I know you will. I'm going now. Think about it like this. It is only a job you do for me. And you are going to pocket richly for a small job."

Luckily, Sylvia was out when he came home. The note said she had to deliver flowers and then she was going to visit her mother. He wrote that he had to see clients and that he would see her the next day.

He hadn't slept that night. He was back in that small, overfull home of his youth with no bright vision in front of him. What hit him the hardest was his impotence. Have you ever heard about such a stupid plan? What can he do? Go to the police and spill the beans? Rothwell will simply laugh at his stupidity. And the penalty clauses? They ripped about everything from him.

Okay, it was just a job for Rothwell. He will do it, take his share of the money and get away. It would clean his record with Rothwell, mind you, he will then have a sword over Rothwell's head. With his share, he would buy his own property, erect buildings and sell it. He will not be at the mercy of others anymore. He made peace with himself and did what Rothwell expected of him.

Only one time they met. Five men in an obscure hotel. The time was fixed and the modus operandi set out. Rothwell suggested that they pool the money and he keeps it safe until the dust settle. They all agreed except Hannes. He wanted his share and vanish and never want to see any one of them again.

"Reconsider it," Rothwell said but didn't insist.

The evening of the bust he parked his truck a few blocks away. With a small bag of equipment, he went to the building. At one side with larger windows than in front, he broke the window and open it wide with gloves on. He wore old tekkies because he knew it wouldn't leave clear tracks. He would, in any case, get rid of them somewhere. He looked around carefully and walked to the front, unlocked it quickly and went in hastily. A few minutes later Rothwell and his friends showed up. Outside a few motorbikes drove noisily to and fro.

"Right." It was Rothwell's signal. The hole should be broken through. In the dim light of a covered flashlight, Hannes hit the last layer as softly as possible. His heart was in his throat, his nerves in tatters. The plaster that come loose falling on the floor sounded like thunder.

And suddenly there was the siren of a police car. He froze and sweat broke out all over his body. He wanted to run. He just didn't know where to. Without taking a breath, he listened. The sirene sounded louder and then rushed by in front of the shop and become softer as it drove away.

Then he did not care anymore. A few heavy swings with the big hammer hit a hole through the last layer and a big hole opened. Someone climbed through and shone with his flashlight. He knew exactly where to get what. Rothwell and the others joined him and Rothwell gestured to them where they should harvest. Six bags they shoved through the opening to Hannes.

It felt like an eternity when they eventually climbed back through the hole. They took off their rubber gloves and put them in the bags. Rothwell for the last time flashed his light through the opening to make sure nothing had been left behind.

"Okay," he said softly, "then we keep everything together." Hannes took his bag and tools. "This is my payment. Go. I will lock up."

The others silently went through the door and vanished into the dark night. Hannes made certain he had all his tools. He wiped the doorknob on the inside as well. It was dead quiet in the streets. But he could swear there are eyes following him. On the corner, he glanced back quickly. No one, but his breath was heavy through his throat.

He went to hide his loot. Thereafter he went to a bar and had a few drinks. When he arrived at Sylvia, she was already in bed.

"Had a nice match?" she asked half asleep. He snorted something like yes and got in the bed next to her. Her caressing body helped to alleviate the tension within him.

She was so excited about the few weeks of leave he was taking. He made the finer touches to the house. Extra paint here and there, varnished the sanded wooden floors and put on cupboard locks. Sometimes he just sat. Tried to think positively. They made a criminal out of him. So far so good. The newspapers reported after a week that there were no suspects, that the owner was on holiday in the Cape, that the builder was on leave after he had finished with the work two weeks before. The possibility of accomplices from within the bank was also investigated.

So, two weeks after the looting, he was in high spirits when he rose. Today was the first day of his real life. Today he wanted to finish off with a few chores and then he and Sylvia can start planning their future.

But that day turned out to be the first day of a hell of eight years.

13 THE FIRST TARGET

Time with Sylvia is simply wonderful but he realizes he will have to go. Maybe one of the police gets it in his head to harass him about the money. He will leave tomorrow and gets his things organized for his revenge. The money keeps him awake at night. If someone thinks that he got to his share, they will come and look for it here at Sylvia's. He wants to avoid that at all costs.

"I must get things organized," is all she gets out of him even if her eyes beg. "I will contact you later, maybe in a month or so. Keep yourself ready for a new life and future with me."

She is heartbroken. Eight years she was alone. Different guys wanted to come closer but she could simply not engage in a relationship. She held on to the wonderful days with Hannes, pampered it and never doubt her great love for him.

Betsy wasn't happy with her bondage especially when she heard about his letter. "Sylvia, you mustn't bind yourself like this. Go out with other men. Maybe he doesn't want you anymore. Years in jail are definitely going to change him."

But she clung to his image, she felt his arms around her and every evening she climbed in bed with hope and dreamt about fiery embraces, his strong body tightly cuddling hers. In the mornings, she always knew she would wait for him. Deep inside her, she never doubts his love for her.

He can start a new life. He has money. She also has somewhat. The boarding house is profitable. They can now start anew. Her thoughts and passion grow like a creeper about a new life with him. She sits next to him on the sofa, kisses his ear. "I don't want to lose you again."

He doesn't react. Only stares at the TV not seeing anything. Somehow, it gives her hope but intuitively she knows she shouldn't say something.

He knows there is no turning around. He packs his suitcase and says goodbye. She is quiet. Before he even exits the driveway, she turns around heartbroken and walks to the house. She wanted to say: 'I love you; come back soon; I'm waiting for you' but she swallows the words with tears welling in her eyes. When do you become free from the rubbish in life that creeps like the tentacles of an octopus around you?

In one of the suburbs, he visits a barber to give him a new look that fits his new passport. He has grown a short beard, neatly trimmed but now a moustache and a wig might be necessary, maybe glasses. Then he drives to the bank they had looted years ago.

At the reception desk, he asks for Van Zyl, his old friend who had worked there. The girl says she doesn't know such a person, but Ms Ina - she is a spinster you know - is an old hand and might have known the man. Her office is down the corridor second last door on the right.

Ms Ina is very helpful. "You know, it was so strange when he suddenly left. It was so eight or ten years ago just after the bank robbery. He was also under suspicion, but let me tell you, everyone in the bank knew he was innocent. It was only that simple bank manager who disliked Boeta. He wanted to get rid of him because he was critical about the rudeness of the manager towards clients. They offered him a separation package. They couldn't fire him because he did nothing wrong. But as I always am saying: the bosses in the banks have too much authority …"

"I agree. Where can I find him?"

She thinks for a while. "Something like Fisher's something… I had to forward his letters … Fish …. Fish …" Then her face lights up. "Oh, yes. Fisher's Post. You know, in the Kalahari Desert. He bought a farm there, I think. Are you going to visit him?"

"Don't know. Maybe it is too far."

"Yes, it is far."

And it was far. Late in the afternoon, he stops at Pofadder, books into the hotel, goes out and buys a bottle of whisky. His room is an outbuilding. He buys some snacks at the general dealer. Then he walks to the post office. In the telephone directory he finds what he is looking for. B.J. van Zyl, Land,'s End and a telephone number. He won't dare to make a call because he knows the telephones lines are all connected at a central place. It can leave a spoor. Other ears, as they say in jail.

Land's End. A crooked sign tells him he is on track. It is even before the little town of Fisher's Post. He asked a few men on their way with goats along the way whether they know such a place. They told him he should watch out on the right-hand side a few kilometres from Fisher's Post.

The sign is old and the letters are almost unreadable from age. He turns off the main road into a winding farm road through the camel thorn trees and sand dunes. The road is not too bad.

About ten kilometres from the turnoff, the surroundings become rockier and there are also a few rocky hills. He starts to move into a sort of canyon. When it is raining, you won't be able to get through, he thinks. Mostly you drive along the lowest part of a river or fountain bed. But it is dry now. No sign of water. The road suddenly swerves from the bottom and climbs up against the low foot of a hill. And suddenly he sees something very cute. A little bridge was built across the centre of the dry bottom. He stops. It's so strange, here in the middle of nowhere, but when he observes the surroundings more carefully, he realises that in reality two dry fountains join here and it was a clever plan to build a bridge here. The path he followed was along with the smaller one, the other one is quite larger and where they connect, the furrow is quite deep. The joining and the shallow exit of water mean that water will dam up here when it rains and this little bridge is just the right thing.

A short distance from the bridge, the world becomes flat and at the end of the plain, he sees at the feet of high dunes amongst camel thorn trees, the home of the owner of Land's End. He gets a fright when he sees Van Zyl.

He remembers something of his face but the body and face are ragged and he looks old. He is not shaven and his face looks shabby. When they eventually sit in the sitting room enjoying coffee and biscuits, Hannes can't help feeling some pity for one of his exploiters. And this is not what he wants to feel. He hoped the man would inflame his hatred, enough so that he can fulfil his promise in court and execute his plans.

"Do you sell insurance or are you a debt collector?" Van Zyl asks suspiciously.

"No, I sell electronic equipment. Shavers and electric toothbrushes and so on." He points at the black small suitcase that he put down on the floor next to the chair.

"But we will have a look on later. How long are you farming here?"

"Eight years." He sighs. Something is bothering him, Hannes realises. But he seems to be quite suspicious and not eager to talk.

"And how is farming here? I mean I am a city boy. I have no idea how to make an existence out of the dry area."

Van Zyl looks out of the front door as if the answer will get to him by looking. "Oh, I'm surviving."

So all the thousands of rands you got from the looting are gone.

"Yes," Van Zyl continues with a flat voice, "after my wife's death a year ago it is difficult for me on the farm."

"But I understand there are rich farmers in this vicinity." Steady now, Hannes. Don't let him close like an oyster.

Van Zyl peeps at him from behind his rough eyebrows. He may be suspicious but he is also greedy for conversation. However, he finds it difficult to be convivial with the stranger.

"Well, if you have enough money, you can farm well, but …." The conversation is more or less at its end. Suddenly Hannes remembers the almost full bottle of whisky in his case. He gets it out.

"Look," he tries to make a joke, "all this sand has given me a mighty thirst. What about a drink or two?"

Van Zyl doesn't answer. He just gets up and brings two glasses and a jug of cold water from the kitchen.

"Ice I haven't got. My fridge is not doing its job properly. Will have to replace it. But the water is cold."

"It is going to be quite nice." He pours two stiff rounds.

"The little bridge out there is a cute piece of work. Did you build it?"

"Yes, and I am quite proud. Earlier after heavy rains, you simply could not get through. Look the two fountains join there and the bigger one can run strongly. Then after the rain, the water is dammed there. That is why I built the bridge. It is marvellous to cross the water when it rains."

"Well, that I can believe." He pours another round and Van Zyl swallows eagerly. They talk about the heat, rain, the lengthy droughts. Whisky does wonders to someone's speech organs.

"You say you must have a lot of money to start a farm here." The crab has come out of his shell nicely.

Van Zyl explains: "The land is not so expensive, but you must buy big to ensure enough pasture for sheep and goats. Small farming doesn't work in this area. And you must have quality livestock. That is one of the principles of successful farming. But it is expensive. A stud ram costs a fortune and you must have a few of those. Mine is too old now for a quality progeny."

Not words of a successful farmer Hannes thinks again. What has gone wrong?

He pours another round. "But eight years back when you bought here, things must have been much cheaper and I suppose you had enough money. You worked somewhere else, not so?" As if farming is not work. He sees some of the suspicion back in Van Zyl's eyes. Steady now!

"No, I mean, I always had a dream of some farm somewhere, but I don't think I will have enough money. You know, Mr Van Zyl, I was a businessman, successful too. But the business world is full of rogues. I didn't play nicely in their game and the guys stripped me naked."

He pours the last of the bottle in Van Zyl's glass. He swallows it without adding water. He is ready to talk.

"Yes, I know of them. I had suffered under them as well." And if he has been waiting for years to tell his story, he continues. "Yes, we were a few guys with an excellent plan. It would make us all independent. One big venture. Each would get his share. The fuckers, they used me, used my knowledge and after this big thing, they kicked my ass and gave me a consolation prize. I had to resign from my work and move over here. The others are stinking rich by now, except for one guy. He sits with his ass somewhere else."

Hannes smiles. No, he is sitting right in front of you.

"Precisely what I mean," Hannes concurs, "they are like hawks. They devour you alive." But he has heard enough. Poor Van Zyl, poor me. The hawks chose their prey wisely and they ate.

They engage in small talk about the weather and politics, but Van Zyl realises that Hannes's conversation has dried up.

"You wanted to show me your things." He gestures to the case but Hannes explains that he now realises that electric equipment won't work on the farm. He must leave now. Van Zyl greets him meekly, relaxed by the alcohol.

He stops on the bridge. Out of the black case, he takes an electric shaver. He switches it on. Then he throws it down the fountain bed and sees how it hops over the sand and explodes in a sand-and-smoke cloud. Enough to bomb away half of a man's face.

Half an hour later, Van Zyl stands thinking deeply in the fountain bed with a piece of distorted plastic in his hand. He shakes his head. Does Hannes think I am a nitwit? Of course, he is Hannes van Velden even with his beard and his false moustache. He immediately recognized him. He knows he played along beautifully. He remembered the words in the court and instinctively knew he was a target.

He watched him as he departed through a window with binoculars. He knew something was going on when Hannes stopped on the bridge.

Slowly a smile forms on his lips. Hannes wants to blow up the looters. He must phone Carl right away. Their day of reckoning has arrived.

Car goes over cliff

Mr Willem Schoonraad, a well-known businessman of Johannesburg, died instantly after a tyre of his car burst and he drove over an abyss. The accident happened late on Friday afternoon near Plettenberg Bay. Mr Schoonraad was on his way to his holiday home in Jeffreys Bay. The road is wellknown for its sharp bends and more than once claimed an awfull toll. A motorist following Mr Schoonraad's car, said he saw something like a little cloud coming from the right hand back tyre after which the car swerved seemingly uncontrollable, went through the safety barrier and over the cliff.

He stopped and saw the car rolling down the rocky decline. It burst out in flames.

According to the police and emergency crew, they had to struggle for a long time to reach the burntout car at the foot of the cliff.

Petrus glances absentmindedly over the report on the front page of the newspaper his attention focused on the door of the grand hotel in one of the suburbs of Johannesburg. Typical story. I think my husband is sleeping around. Watch him. Report confidentially to me only.

He hates it.

But money is money. You need money to live. And this is what Karin wants. She can't get enough of it. And he is being paid. Thousands. No questions asked about his fee. He must bring results. That he does.

His automatic camera clicks continuously when the pair comes out of the hotel. Side by side, they walk arm in arm down the stairs that lead to the parking area.

In the parking area, a taxi is awaiting him. She kisses him passionately, hugs him tightly, caresses his dark hair and their hands clutch until he climbs into the taxi. She loiters to the garden, plucks a rose and sticks it in her hair. Then she vanishes around the corner of the hotel.

He hates this work with a fiery hatred. To sit and wait in a car for hours just to take photos of an extramarital affair was never his idea of detective work. But Karin insisted. A detective in the service earns too little, she argued continuously. You can earn ten times your salary with private work. Someone with your talents cannot waste his time with routine police work.

She was correct halfway. Police remuneration was horrible. They had to reside in an average suburb. By the day, Karin became more grumpy. Like a sun beetle, she sang the same maddening song, especially after the case of the bank robbery that he so brilliantly solved.

He resigned and started his own practice. He was amazed at the reaction to his advertisement. So many rich people with so many things to find out or to hide. Not long thereafter, they could move to a better suburb and after his father's death, he could with his inheritance and the profit on his home, build in an upper-class suburb. Double storey, swimming pool, big family room, name it. That gave him some consolation. He became something more than his previous colleagues, more than routine detective work.

But this sort of thing he loathes. He hates infidelity because it is such a part of his life. At this moment, he is entrapped. His work pays for his expensive home, his expensive car, his expensive wife.

He switches on the car and drives home. The sun lies low on the horizon in the west.

He will develop the photos tomorrow and report to his client.

Arriving at home, he finds Karin and Stefan in the kitchen. Stefan is sitting on his toddler's stool covered with chocolate ice cream.

"Hello, Dad!" Karin calls exuberantly, "look how I ate and smeared myself!" She scratches over Stefan's head and ruffles his hair. "Look how your snout looks. Dad won't even want to kiss you."

The day's dismay vanishes. Karin can suddenly change the world into a fairy dream. He comes nearer and kisses Stefan through the chocolate on a wet, laughing mouth.

"You little rascal. I will have you to take etiquette lessons. Sis, what a mess," he laughs.

He tickles the boy under his arms. Stefan yells out of pleasure.

"Come, let's get you into the bath en bed. This is where sweet little boys belong." She winks at Petrus, grabs Stefan out of his stool and goes to the bathroom. Petrus walks to the sitting room and opens a bottle of Shiraz. Karin likes Shiraz. When he sits down on the sofa, he can hear Stefan's loud shrieks of joy.

When she, later on, sits with her glass of wine in her hand, cuddling close and irresistibly to him, she whispers: "I missed you today."

Karin! Karin! I can't keep you, but I also can't lose you! You spook me. I'm like a prisoner. Your net is tightly woven around me and you can do what you want with me.

"I'm going to shower," she says a little later. "Don't let me wait too long for you." She winks at him and goes up the stairs leading to their suite. He only shakes his head and smiles. Then he relaxes against the cushion. Yes, the bank robbery made a big difference in his life. It was sort of a crossroads.

He was elated when the case was given to him. He was young, intelligent, and enthusiastic. With Karin's nagging and also hungry for recognition and promotion, he gave in. Some nice detective work, rather routine work he had done meticulously, led to the apprehension of a few terrible crooks. One of them was the cunning and elusive Carl Greeff. This brought him to the attention of the bosses in the detective squad. Carl's capture for him was a mighty pleasure. For days, he watched an obscure bar. He had only a vague inclination that Carl might visit the place. He smiles when he thinks about Carl's amazement when he confronted him. He looked at Petrus with big eyes in a pale face. He was so surprised that he surrendered and cuffed Petrus led him to his car.

The commander told him that this case was a big challenge for such a young man, because of skimpy clues. Maybe it could be an inside job. Rothwell is the owner of the building at the back of the bank.

The name Rothwell hit him in the chest. In the world of fraud, bribing, and blackmail the name wasn't unfamiliar. But he was inviolable. Even if many knew or had a suspicion of his involvement, or even that he was the brain behind the misconduct, they could not lay a finger on him. He covered his tracks so well and in time wiped it out long before one could attach any mischief to him. And he had a shrewd attorney.

Rothwell's building. He considered the facts: the time the building was empty; the perfect planning and execution of the robbery; the fact that all tracks were wiped out; that Rothwell and Hannes had watertight alibis. It was too good to be true. Rothwell! Yes, this time Mr R will see his ass.

It was easier said than done. All the suspects kept to their alibis. The suspect in the bank simply said he knew nothing. He is supposed to retire one of these days. Why would he do something like this and jeopardize his pension? Rothwell was out of town. Hannes' girl said she had visited her mother. Hannes was at a rugby match. When she got home, she went to bed at maybe ten. Shortly after that, he arrived smelling of alcohol. She was already half asleep. It was rugby, and afterwards the guys went to the bar. That's all. The bartenders said there were so many people they couldn't remember each one. Dead end.

Petrus sat hours sifting through data about Rothwell. Newspaper clips, police records, and all the affidavits from people mainly around Hannes and Rothwell. But he also came across Rothwell's close associates. Schoonraad, rich with properties all over the place. His attorney, Rhoode, one of the best known and most capable attorneys in South Africa. His case against Rothwell, if there was a case, should be watertight. No public prosecutor would dare to prosecute Mr R on shaky testimonies in court.

Back to the building and the missing millions. No money, no witnesses, nothing.

For the umpteenth time, he visited the building. Somewhere must be something. What is he missing? Checking the window from the outside. It was broken from the outside. Tracks. No, the rain washed it away. Then inside. At the back of the building. Tracks, yes. All spoors of ancient takkies. Fingerprints? There would be none. This was meticulously planned.

He was standing in the middle of the room when he saw it. No footprints on the inside next to the window. Shit!

"Constable," he shouted elated. "Go outside and climb through the window."

"What?"

"Please, go outside and climb through the window as if you were a burglar. I want to see what happens."

The constable shook his head. At the window, he had some difficulty opening it through the hole in the windowpane. He also had some difficulty in getting himself on the frame. It wasn't so high that you should struggle but also not so low that you can walk through. On the windowsill, the constable sat on his hunches and then he jumped. Dust whirled up from under his shoes.

"Eureka!" Petrus bellowed, "I've got it. No one came through the window. The door was opened after someone had broken the window from outside as an eye blind."

"What?"

"Look where you have landed, you made prominent tracks in the dust? Do you see any others like yours?"

The constable shook his head.

Rothwell! He has keys. He simply had to get more information.

He zoomed in on Mr R.

Why was the building erected? Why suddenly on holiday during the robbery? Who else had keys to the building? Who else was on the job? How did you know the alarms wouldn't go off? Who was the accomplice in the bank?

He was so convinced it was Rothwell, he decided on a nerve war. Time and again he visited him. More questions. More affidavits to cover particulars. Rubbish like: how long did the building take to finish; who drew the plans; could the drawer perhaps got hold of the keys; who else was helping with the project; and so on.

Rhoode, like a shadow, was present each time. In the end, he threatened to get a court order preventing Petrus to harass Rothwell. It is then that he played his ace.

"I won't bother you again. I think I have enough to move on with the case." He could see that his words worried them. "Good night, gentlemen." He had nothing, only a sure conviction that Rothwell was his man.

And then, out of the blue, a breakthrough. "Go and talk to Jan Diergaardt," the man told him. "I saw in the newspaper there are no suspects yet. Jan was in the bar last night full of stories about what he saw the night of the burglary. I thought I just tell you. Evenings he sits in the Royal Hotel's bar." The guy that stopped him on the pavement quickly vanished in between the crowds going home after work.

Jan wasn't a reliable witness but he was the only one. In court, he would collapse. However, for a drink or two, Jan sang and whistled.

"Sir, look. I know I always take a drink or two too many. But that evening, I had a terrible stomach ache and could not drink so much. About ten that evening I quit and walked home. I had to pass there where they were building. But I am on the opposite of the street. About a block or what I saw the cab alone in the street. And I thought: why is this thing standing here. They will steal the thing. But I walked further and when I was opposite the building, my bladder called out loudly. I had to pee. I slipped into a narrow corridor. And then I saw a man coming out of the building with a bag. He locked the door and walked down to his cab. He got in the thing and drove off. I first thought the guy had to work late but when the oaks in the bar told me about the bank robbery, I thought, yes, it was the builder's truck, because I passed there many times when they were still building. I could swear it is the same truck. If you catch the guy and get the money back, will the bank give me some?"

He was convinced that even if Jan hadn't lied, it was not the work of one person, but it was a start. The builder could have been part and parcel of the plan. Yes, he had a key and could freely come and go as he pleased.

On a good Monday morning, he took Hannes van Velden into custody. He hoped under pressure Hannes would crack and divulge the whole thing. The newspapers praised his fine detective work. His boss was satisfied.

Hannes didn't give in. Monotolously he clung to his story. Rothwell told the press that he generously would provide legal representation for Hannes because he was working for him.

He sent Rhoode to Hannes.

Suddenly there is a knock on his door.

Annoyed Hannes looks away from the interesting TV show he is watching. What else can you do in a lonely hotel room? He rises and opens the door. The little man stands in front of him.

"Smiley said you must come. Jakkie escaped from jail."

He is gone before Hannes can utter a word.

Smiley is highly agitated. His awkward body moves continuously on his stump legs. When Jemima peeps around the corner, he chastises her with a flood of words so that she instantly vanish.

"The damn Jakkie! He is now going to see his ass. Either the cops or his enemies will find him. If the others find him, it is tickets with him. Knife. That's all."

"How can I help?"

"You must think carefully. You knew him well. He talked with you many times. Did he ever mention escape?"

Hannes thinks deeply. "No, never."

"Jakkie had a few pals. Fuck man, think! Did he mention any names? Did he ever tell you what he and his mates have done?"

Stress causes sweat to run in streams over Smiley's fat face. "If I just could lay my hands on him first …"

Hannes tries to remember. Well, stories in jail are stories. You hear it, laugh about it and forget it. Mostly it is rubbish. Stories from imaginative, criminal brain cells. Mostly about a hero figure against a miserable world. An endeavour to turn the badass side of the world around.

Hannes just shakes his head.

"Give him a drink!" Smiley yells at the little man. "Can't you see he is thirsty? I must get to Jakkie before shit hits him. They will cut out his intestines."

Now tears run over his fat cheeks.

Then something hits Hannes. It was the story of Jakkie and his car mates. It was years ago, but something of the daring in the plan stayed with him.

"Wait. Let me see! He and his mates stole cars. Many of them. Buy that evening one of them pretended to be a lackey at a smart hotel where there was a function for important guests. The people came with their expensive cars. I think it was Jakkie himself that was supposed to drive and park the cars somewhere. He then drove down the street and handed the car to one of his mates. The mate then parked the car elsewhere. So they stole six cars that night."

He remembers it now more clearly. What did Jakkie say? It was quite funny. He plays with the glass in his hand. Vanish … vanish …

Suddenly he smiles. "Smiley, I've got it. Dorie. Do you know Dorie? Jakkie said: Me and Dorie, and Flippie –yes, I think it was Flippie, did the vanishing trick. When the party was over, we had already vanished with six cars."

Smiley relaxes slightly. "Flippie is no more. He was shot by the police when he ran away. Dorie sat a few years for stealing cars but he is out now. Come, I think I am going to need you."

Through the back door and the storeroom, they reach the garage. A shiny, black Mercedes awaits them. Moments later, they are on their way to the Vaal River. The little man drives fast and dexterous. Smiley is using his cellphone and making one call after the other. Hannes tries to follow the conversations but it is highly coded in one or other gang language.

"They are looking for Jakkie. The police think they know where he is. The family of the guy who he knifed is also after his blood. Also, the guys whom he crooked out of cars and money! Put your foot down on that petrol! Do you want us to stand still? Hell, I worry me to death. That little brother of mine will send me straight to hell. Real scoundrel, that Jakkie."

Before the bridge over the Vaal, they take a right turn all along the river. "Look out for a sign Twilight. They say Dorie will be there in his old hangout."

And probably Jakkie also. Once again Hannes is amazed at the underground's excellent communication systems. No wonder they are yards ahead of the police most of the time

Twilight is an almost unrecognizable, skew sign. There is an iron gate with a lock which the little man unlocks in seconds with a piece of wire.

The path has not been used recently. The track is overgrown and at places invisible in the dimmed car lights. They drive slowly and hobble down the decline to the river. In front of them, they see a cluster of trees and bushes. They stop and climb out.

Smiley hands over a torch to Hannes. "Go and see if you can find anything. Talk to him. If he hears I am with you, he will run away."

"Why?"

"That's another story. Please, go and search for Jakkie before the cops get here. Be careful, they could have some firearm with them."

Hannes swiftly moves towards the first trees and shrubs. When the car's lights become too dim, he switches on the torch. About fifty meters of open space lies in front of him. He switches off the torch and in the dim starlight, cautiously moves in between the trees and shrubs. Just as he wants to switch on the torch again, he sees a flickering through the bushes. A few steps further and the flickering disappears. Bushes in front of him. Stealthily he advances trying to avoid branches that he cannot see and feels his way forward.

Suddenly he sees the flickering again. The decline is now steeper and he has to move step-by-step. A dry branch crackles under his foot in the silent night. Ten yards from a fire almost burnt out he stops. No sound. Then suddenly the hoo-hoo of an owl and wings snap the silence in pieces. He freezes. Are they watching him? Is a revolver already aiming at his heart?

Can they see him? Must he call out for Jakkie? Suddenly there is a thundering sound from his righthand side. It sounds like the snorting of a rhino. And then another one cueing in with the first.

Hannes smiles relieved. No sudden piece of lead in his ribs. He knows what the sounds are. He switches on the torch and moves in the direction of the sounds. Under a tree, on a bed of leaves, he sees two empty bottles of brandy.

Next to it lie the two bodies on their backs, with open mouths in a snoring match.

He turns around and jogs to Smiley. Quickly he enlightens them.

"We must be quick. I shall carry Jakkie. You can carry Dorie."

They were scarcely back on the tarred road when a police van with a flashing blue light comes down the road at high speed. When Hannes looks back he just sees the stoplights of the police van coming on before it turned off.

"Foot in the corner! Fuck it, we nearly saw our asses. The fucking Jakkie, tonight I'll fuck him up."

The mighty engine of the Mercedes let them fly over the road on their way back to Johannesburg.

Somewhere in a suburb, they stop in front of a house. They carry Dorie out and dropped him in front of the door. Smiley waits until Hannes is back in the car. He knocks loudly on the front door. Then he turns around and hastens to the car. "Drive!"

When the door opens, they were gone. "His family can look after him," says Smiley simply.

There is no way in which Hannes can get back to his hotel now. Smiley is too thankful and wants to compensate. While Jakkie lies in the corner of Smiley's luxurious sitting room watched by the little man, Smiley treats Hannes to the most expensive French champagne in South Africa.

"Thanks," he says repeatedly. "This is a wonderful thing you did for me tonight."

Smiley amazes him. He didn't do much. Okay, if it wasn't for the brandy, things could have turned out quite differently. But what did Smiley mean that Jakkie would run away? And where on earth did he find this heavenly champagne?

Smiley is eager to talk. Now that the tension is gone that Jakkie could be apprehended, he is quite jovial.

"I'm glad you like it. It is the best, superb. And so easily and for nothing acquired. We got a guy at the customs gambling and cheated him badly. Then we threaten him that we will cut his guts out if he didn't pay up. We kept on the pressure and when he thought he was completely fucked, we said we want that champagne he told us about. He organised everything and we arrived with papers he gave us and collect it and drive out again. And I tell the man at the checkpoint I was so impressed with their security, they are top men. And the guy was so flattered he stamped the papers again. So we drink double stamped champagne ..."

His laugh roars through the room. "Jakkie and I will finish a bottle or two." Tears well in his eyes. "My little brother, my Jakkie, the little shit ..."

He wipes with his hand over his mouth, combs with his fingers through his hair, pours another round.

"I swear he won't know tomorrow where he is. My goodness, he could be in a cell. And this time they won't spare him. Those sticks they carry break one's ribs and if he gets an arm in front...," Smiley shivers, "... he is so small and soft. You know, I am his elder brother, but I am also his father and mother. We never knew our parents, always from one orphanage to the other. Then people came and wanted to part us, each one to different foster parents. Then I said: never, you don't take Jakkie from me. He's got nothing; only me. Then during the night we ran away and looked for other lodging and when he cried I comforted him and when he cried too much, I hit him. So I brought him up. He really is a child to me."

There are tears of compassion in his eyes when he looks at the pathetic bundle on the floor.

"But, I say thank you again. Let's have another bottle. You are truly now one of my chums. Tell me everything about yourself."

They chat until sunrise. It was nice for Hannes to talk about everything in such a relaxed atmosphere.

"Come Friday evening for a drink. Then you can speak to Jakkie as well."

"Thanks, Smiley. But I can't. Must be in Knysna for a very important thing."

Today he is irritated to no end. He has been sitting for hours in his hot car in the burning sun. There is no movement from the hotel's entrance. He should have bought a newspaper this morning. This one on the seat next to him is an old one. Terribly bored, he pulls the newspaper nearer and read the rest of the story about the accident near Jeffreys.

"According to the cab's driver, the car went down over the cliff, and when he stopped, he could hear the explosion as the car took fire. It was a horrible experience. What he couldn't understand, was that the man in a BMW who was parked under a tree at a stopover, only about fifty meters from the crash, drove off in the direction of Knysna. He should have seen the accident."

Petrus suddenly sits erect, his detective brain full steam at work. Schoonraad and Jeffreys Bay connects. He had to drive to Jeffreys to get Schoonraad's, a close friend of Rothwell's, story. At that time, he had a strong suspicion that Schoonraad has a finger in the pie of the bank robbery. He forces himself to think systematically. When was it? Seven, eight years back. Before he resigned. There were other suspects as well. Someone from the bank, but Rothwell was the main suspect. That was when he roped in Hannes van Velden. That was when he became a hero.

Won't the pair please come out of the hotel! He has been sitting here for hours and he is depressed. This time it's the wife of a stinking rich man who thinks her husband is dating one or another slut. He has a photo of the man and he followed him from his office. On the other side of the double door of the hotel, he could see how they embrace. But it won't be a good photo. That's why he waits patiently.

Schoonraad and Jeffreys Bay. He picks up his cell phone.

Lucia answers.

"Hello, my favourite niece," he tries to sound sweet.

"Petrus, you low, dirty pig. Why don't I hear anything from you for months? Earlier when you were in the force, you pitched up regularly. Now …"

"Lucie, my darling. When I worked for the state, I used their time. Nowadays I must use my own time and time is money, you know?"

"Feeble apology. You don't fool me. And I've got so much to tell you."
He and Lucy had always been close and she is the social butterfly of the
century.

"I promise …"

She laughs heartily. "That I've heard before. What do you want this
time?"

Lucia works at the archive of a newspaper. She knows about computers
and data.

"Seven or eight years ago I sent a man to jail after a bank robbery.
Hannes van Velden. There were probably accomplices but I could not find
anything against them. I'm looking for all those guys' names, please."

"Okay. I'll phone you back. What are you doing?"

"Sitting in front of a hotel waiting for my client's husband who plays
around with another girl. Has been sitting here the whole bloody morning.
They sure take their time."

"How romantic," she guys. "Okay, phone you back in a few minutes."

A very slow half an hour passes.

Then the long, dark man comes through the double doors with a cute
brunet hanging on his arm. His cell phone rings. Damn!

He switches it on and puts it in the holder. While he gets his camera
ready, he speaks: "Lucie, is it you? I'll phone you back shortly. The guy and
his girl have just come out of the hotel. I must take photos."

"No, you don't phone me back. Keep on your phone and tell me what's
happening, right? It sounds so exciting." Lucie flourishes on sensation.

"Okay, they are on the steps now. I focus my camera. Good, they are
nicely in the picture. Zoom in a bit. Fine. Now I push the button for a
photo. They are now standing next to each other talking, saying goodbye
probably. He wants to turn around to leave but it looks as if she wants to
say something to him. Push the button. Now, u-la-la, she storms him and
get her arms around his neck and kisses him. Now I hold on to the button
and take a lot of pictures."

He concentrates so intensely that he stops talking. "And now?" Lucie's
voice is hoarse from exhilaration.

"Now he kisses her, or rather they are kissing each other. And, as you
read in romantic fiction: passionately. Okay, I've got what I wanted. He has
seen his ass."

"What are they doing now?"

"They are still kissing. There, he leaves her now, looking at his watch. He says something and then departs at high speed. Gallivanted too long? He walks quickly to the parking area."

"And she?"

"Still standing there. Bloody beautiful."

"How does she look?"

"Longish, perfect body with brown hair. Quite cute, I would say. Oh, she is waiting for a taxi. She gets in. End of story."

"What now?"

"I'm going to develop the photos, put them in an envelope and hand it over to my client together with my invoice. She pays me and I have nothing further to do with it. The photos are quite enough proof if she wants a divorce. This sort of thing doesn't end up in court nowadays. Usually, the attorneys take care of everything."

"Shame, poor woman!"

"Remember, this is only one side of the story. Usually, it is far more complicated. But leave that for now. Have you ..."

"Shame. Yes, I have. It was eight years ago. The guys were Van Zyl, a bank clerk from the looted bank, Schoonraad, a rich businessman from Johannesburg and close associate of Rothwell the main suspect, and the builder Hannes van Velden. He was sentenced to ten years in prison. Nothing of the 'several million' has been found. The only witness was Jan Diergaardt. Rothwell's attorney, Rhoode, was Van Velden's defence lawyer. That is that in short. If you are interested..."

"... then I come and visit you and get all the information. I promise ..."

"Empty promise. But you are welcome. Wait, I must go. I've got a mean boss."

"Hang on a bit. Is the Schoonraad of the motor accident and Schoonraad, the suspect, the same person?"

"I'll check. See you later."

Good. His memory is now properly refreshed. Eight years he nourishes the memory of the case but the finer detail seems to subside. He made his name with that one. Now he starts to meticulously reconstruct the detail. And then the scene in the court comes into his mind. How could he forget that! Hannes declined to say anything in court except 'I am innocent. He had, after being sentenced to jail, when they took him out, turned around, his face white with emotion. "I shall get you," almost unhearable through his tight lips. "Each one of you."

He now remembers that their eyes met for a split of a second. That cold, stealy look in his eyes!

He didn't worry about that then. The sentence was his personal triumph. And further, there are many guys sentenced to jail that throw one or other threat against the system and those who were responsible for his misfortune.

Van Zyl, Van Velden, Schoonraad, Rothwell. He munches the names. And maybe Schoonraad gone. If the car didn't burn out, the forensic investigation could be so much easier. Was it really a tyre burst? What about the white BMW? Something doesn't fit.

But then he must curb his imagination. Hannes was sentenced to ten years in jail. Lucie says it was eight years ago. Hannes is probably safely behind bars at this moment but he could also be out on parole.

He can't shake it off. Those cold eyes suddenly stay in his mind. He sees him in his mind's eye when he apprehended him, probably more or less the same age as himself. He stubbornly stuck to his alibi even when he was threatened with witnesses. Petrus is now is sure the threat of Hannes in court include him.

When he picks up his son at his mother, he knows he must find out. This is a loose end.

He remains restless during the whole evening. Karin was tired and early went to bed. Stefan is also sleeping. First, he develops the photos in his darkroom. Beautiful pictures. Then he pours a whisky and sits down in the sitting room. He will get to Hannes' case in the morning. Jasper Vermeulen, his old colleague and a rugby pal in their younger days, is still in the police force.

The next morning he phones Jasper.

"Jasper, what's on your program. I'll stick you a beer at ten at our old spot."

"Hang Petrus, this is a nice surprise. I wanted to phone you anyway. Maybe you can help me. You know this murder …"

"Let's talk about that later, my friend. Please do me a hell of a favour. You know that guy, Hannes van Velden, that I roped in for the bank robbery eight years ago. Is he still in jail or on parole? Can you find out for me, please?"

"No problem. Where is he? Pretoria?"

"Jip. And that murder you are talking about. I followed it in the newspapers."

"Yes, but something doesn't fit. The guy that is in custody is too obvious the culprit. I suspect …"

"In the meantime, I will think about it. At ten then."

"Okay. See you."

He drops Stefan at the nursery. It is time to visit his client. He hates it. Karin, Karin, do you have an idea what you are doing to me!

Mrs Rhoode is a long, attractive woman with long black hair. Maybe fifty but her care let her look like a woman of forty. When she opens the door, Petrus can only stare at her in amazement. She wears an expensive necklace; diamonds twinkle in the earrings. Fingers with rings of agates, sapphires, and diamonds. She invites him gallantly to enter.

"Coffee? Tea?"

He prefers coffee. It is going to be an uneasy conversation. They engage in small talk while waiting for the coffee. There is a palpable tension in the air. He wishes he could take his briefcase and walk away. He is well and able to face crime, but voyeurism not!

"Madam," he starts unsure when he puts the empty cup in the saucer.

For a moment, she says nothing and only let her eyes drop. "I didn't expect good news," she says softly. "Give me the details. The sooner the better."

He takes the photos out of it his case and hands it over. "This was taken yesterday afternoon at the Masonic Hotel. They were inside quite a few hours. I jotted down all the particulars in the report."

He also hands over his full report to her. Now comes the moment that he loathes the most. Some of them burst into tears, some go in a hysterical frenzy and then he must try to calm them down, others just sit flabbergasted and then he must give advice.

However, Mrs Schoonraad stoically hides her real feelings.

"Thank you, Mr Odendaal. You did excellent work. I've suspected this much."

She remains cool and collected.

"Actually I am relieved," she says smiling dryly. "I have been suspecting for years that he has extramarital affairs. He has also started to hint at divorce, but I suspect he is busy with a game to ensure that I get almost nothing from the divorce. He is a brilliant lawyer, you know."

"I am sorry, Madam," he says clumsily.

"Thanks, I am sorry too. Something like this always is sad and unpleasant. But now you have put the axe in my hands. And I can chop as I please."

She rises and walks to a little table with a drawer. She takes out an envelope. "Thank you very much for your excellent work. Here is R5000. No, don't hesitate to take it. It is some of his money of which he has thousands."

"Is there something else I can do for you?"

"If there is, I'll contact you, thanks. My brother in law is an advocate. We will take it from here."

Her slender hand is cool in his. In her eyes, he can see some dreariness and a look into his without seeing anything.

While he is driving to the club to meet Jasper he thinks and smiles sourly. If he must subpoena Karin who openly commits adultery, what hen? How complicated can life be?

There I still a half an hour before he expects Jasper. No problem. He's got some reports to write.

***

"My mate!" Jasper is a big fellow and always thunderous. He grabs his beer and swallows it as if it is the last bottle in the country. "Now, this is nice. And I can drink as much as I want because I am not officially on duty."

He sits down at the table. Petrus has put his notes in his briefcase. What a nice meeting this is going to be!

"How's everyone at the office?" Petrus still has an intense yearning for his work as a detective.

"It is going well, my mate, quite good." Jasper's voice bellows through the room. "Except that we work ourselves to death. No new appointments are being made. If someone goes, the workload just gets distributed amongst the rest. But I don't complain. All our pals are still there and we enjoy working together."

His last words are sort of an insinuation. He has always been very fond of Petrus.

"And Skinny?"

Jasper laughs heartily while he pours the golden brown bear in his glass. "Well, he still is our boss. Become leaner by the day. Billyboy one day said: one of these days when the door opens and no one comes in, you must know it is Skinny."

They laugh with gusto at the joke. "But he isn't a bad guy and a fair boss."

Then he looks earnestly at Petrus.

"Look, you wanted to know about Hannes van Velden. My mate, he's out."

"What?"

"Amnesty."

"Amnesty?"

"Yes, man. Don't be stupid. The state president gave general amnesty to guys who are no danger to society. Bank robbers, fraudsters, and so on. A few weeks ago. He is one of them. Guys with good records. Seemingly rehabilitated completely."

"What are you telling me!"

"What is behind your enquiry?" Jasper's natural detective suspicion is now alive.

"Maybe. I don't know what or how. This is flabbergasting news. Have to think about it."

He beckons the waiter. Time for another round.

"You have now fuelled my curiosity to no end."

"I know, but give my brain a little chance to get the ducks in a row. In the meantime, tell me your story."

Jasper puts down his glass. Then he starts to turn the glass around with his fingers looking intently at the contents.

"The case of the Morris murder. Look, it looks so easy. They trapped the guy with the knife within half an hour after the girl was killed. A neighbour phoned the police when he heard a noise. The guy's hands are full of blood from the aspiring beauty queen Ms Morris. It was after a party. She was taken home by her agent after a competition she took part in. The accused seemingly followed them because there was a huge fight during the competition."

"Why did he think something was going to happen. I mean why did he follow them?"

"The guy is manic, man. He is so in love with this girl he has followed her everywhere. He looked after her like a baby. And he was jealous, he admitted himself. He said the agent suddenly left the building and passed him in a hurry where he was hiding behind some shrubs in the building's garden. Now, this is true. I checked and his tracks are clear. He then went up to her flat. The door was closed. He knocked but there was no answer. He tried the knob and opened the door. She lied there with a dagger sticking out of her chest. He could see there was no life left in her. He pulled out the dagger and bewildered and shocked only sat there until the police arrived."

"Wow! And the agent?"

"That's one thing worrying me. You know how it works. They arrest a guy, go to the police station. Interrogate him for hours. When they later checked, they found the agent in a bar where he seemingly had sat the whole evening from the time he left the girl's flat. No one can certify how long he sat there. Denies that he knows anything. She was alive when he left after they had a huge argument. He decided to send her to hell, idiomatically speaking. She is too fickle. But sorry about her death. And if he may add, probably that jealous guy, Thomas Black, who followed and pestered her day and night. As far as he knows, she had no other enemies."

"So, it was Blackie or the agent. Time rules out other killers."

"Yes," Jasper concurs. "Between the departure of the agent and the discovery of the corps, there would be little time for someone else to commit the murder. Except when they both are blatant liars. Then maybe…"

They both nod. Petrus thinks about a modus operandi.

"You know what to do. Give him hell!"

"I have, and he is really sort of a softie, but he keeps at his story. I can't catch him out. What is more, when I look at the affidavits of witnesses, everything seems to be against him. Everyone testifies about his consuming jealousy, of how he pestered her about day and night, even made scenes when she was with someone else. How he threatened to kill everyone who comes near her. But somehow …"

"Somehow?"

"It is too obvious. Something is wrong. But if you have no advice, I will somehow sort it out. Okay, back to your story."

"First, another beer." He gestures at the waiter. "My mate, maybe my mind is totally fogged up."

"Makes two of us," Jasper smiles and takes a swig.

"Have you read about it?"

"Schoonraad?"

"Yes, the rich Johannesburg businessman that went over the abyss near Jeffreys. It was in the newspapers."

"Yes, I remember but it didn't ring a bell. Who was he?"

"Maybe the same Schoonraad who was one of the suspects together with Hannes van Velden in the bank robbery eight years ago. The one I solved so brilliantly," he smiles sourly.

"And now Van Velden is free and Schoonraad drives over a cliff. What about it?"

"The guy who saw the accident talked about a white BMW parked nearby and he was wondering how the driver couldn't see the accident because he drove off. He is convinced the driver should have seen it. It is strange. Just imagine …"

"Stop! I am sure you are imagining things."

"No, listen! The day when he was sentenced Van Velden swore almost inaudible that he would get them one by one. What if …"

"If Schoonraad was guilty also, you fucked up badly," Jasper laughs.

"Maybe I had. You said a while ago something I must think about thoroughly. Maybe the whole case was like this. Van Velden wouldn't confess anything and there was only one witness. It was Van Velden who build the thing and had the opportunity to break through the wall. Although Rothwell was my main suspect because it was his building. And when I leaned on Rothwell, suddenly there was a witness. Easy."

"Yes, but according to the guys at the jail, Van Velden was a super inmate. No problems. Even didn't want parole. Why would he now?"

"Remember no money has ever been found."

"Okay. And now he is looking for his share. And you have a faint inkling that Van Velden could have done something to Schoonraad's car."

"I don't know. And it will not easily be determined. The car burnt out."

"Yes, then it is touch and go. It will take a long time for such an investigation and then I doubt it that forensics will find something useful."

"Seem to me the following weeks we are going to be quite busy." He swallows the last drop of beer from his glass.

"You tell me. Something I can help with?"

"I am not sure. Oh, there is something. Try to locate the guy that worked in the bank, Van Zyl."

Lucie can't believe her luck when suddenly he visits her office.

"My lost nephew!" She yells out and then kisses him all over. That's one thing of Lucie. When she does a thing, she doesn't hold back. But it is nice to see her again.

"I also longed for you."

"Damn liar, you," she laughs, "but I'm glad to see you. Let me just finish the letter then I stick you for coffee in our canteen. They can do for a while without me. And our business is official, not so?" She winks at him while her fingers flutter over the letters.

In the canteen, they engage in small talk. How the families are, whether they have much work and so on.

"How's that case coming on?"

"No go. I want to ask you a favour."

"And that's the reason you are here," she laughs.

"No, I really missed you and now that I see you again, I realize we must get together more often"

"Okay, anything for you. By the way, Schoonraad is Willem Schoonraad and the same guy from eight years back, now late Willem Schoonraad."

"Lucie!" He tries to scold her but she holds her hand up.

"Sorry, sometimes my tongue is faster than my brain. What else?"

"The eyewitness of Schoonraad's accident. I want to contact him badly."

"It won't be too difficult. I think it was our reporter in George who wrote the piece. Let's go to my office." Ten minutes later, he has the information.

While he is still with Lucie, his cellphone rings. It is Jasper.

"Listen, it's almost five. I will be at the club in ten minutes. If you are interested in exciting news, join me and buy me a beer."

"Lucie, my girl. Things are picking up. Do you still write reports?"

"Only when a scoop falls in my lap. The other guys do the hard work."

"I promise you. You will be the first person to know of this thing if it isn't an empty shell." He kisses her and hastes himself to the club.

"Hang, Petrus. We must do this frequently. Free beer isn't to be sneezed at."

"Your stomach is becoming too big from all the beer you devour," Petrus teases. "But for this one, I'll pay gladly. So, spit it out."

"Firstly, Van Zyl. He resigned soon after the bank robbery and is now farming in the Kalahari near Fisher's Post. According to the police there he is a quiet guy, no troubles. They know him well. I don't have his telephone number but you will easily get it."

Petrus nods. "It will mean one will have to drive to the Kalahari to talk to him."

"About what?"

"I don't know now. And the other news?"

Jasper wipes over his moustache.

"Wow! Hot news, I'm telling you. Mrs Schoonraad phoned this morning. She spoke to Jamie. She said one of the girls at the office phoned her to enquire about the damage the fire inflicted on the house at Jeffreys. The girl said the caretaker had phoned her to warn Schoonraad about the fire. The girl said with the shocking news of Schoonraad's accident, she had forgotten about the fire. Mrs Schoonraad said she knows nothing about a fire."

"What did the caretaker say?"

"Jamie followed it up. The caretaker said he knew nothing about a fire. He didn't phone the office."

"And now?"

"Jamie will do the ordinary routine investigation for Mrs Schoonraad. Try to find out from which number the call came. Try to locate the owner of the phone, probably a cellphone. You know the drill."

"Jasper, what does all this tell you?"

"I don't know. It looks suspicious."

"And if you put together the facts of the white BMW and Schoonraad's probable part in the bank robbery and the fact that Van Velden is out of jail?"

"Wait a minute! You are losing me."

"Van Velden swore he would get everyone, me included. What if he sabotaged Schoonraad's car. What if it is the first one he killed? Do you know what it means?"

"What?"

"A few murders in the days ahead. And my life is in danger."

"Goodness, you are right! But maybe your suspicions are too farfetched. Maybe there is a simple reason for the accident. Maybe Van Velden has no part in anything."

"And if he has?

"Then it is a bugger up. I shall have a talk with Jamie. We will see what we can do. I'll keep you in the loop. What are you going to do?"

"Don't know yet. Will let you know."

Before he reaches home, he has decided. He drives to Sylvia's boarding house. He can read the disappointment when she opens the door.

"Can I help," she says bluntly.

"Sorry to bother you. Maybe you don't remember me. I was the detective who took Hannes in custody eight years ago. I hear he is out."

"Police?" she asks suspiciously. He ignores the question.

"I want dearly to contact him. Maybe he can help me with another case," he lies fluently. "He wasn't here maybe?"

"He was, but he's gone now. No idea where. No idea if I'll ever see him again. Sorry, I can't help you."

The oyster closes. Conversation closed. The door slams in his face. No go.

While he drives away, he tries to plan his next step. The witness? Maybe not a bad plan. Mrs Schoonraad? He can't visit her officially. The police have probably already visited her for a statement.

"Karin, I'm going to George for a few days." Stefan has already gone to bed.

"Until when?"

He knows what she means. It is in the middle of the week and on Friday night she will have one of her obscure parties.

"I should be back on Saturday. I shall appreciate it if you don't attend your party."

She doesn't answer, but her body language screams. "For the sake of Stefan and for the sake of my mother."

She looks at him questioningly.

"People are already talking behind our backs. Don't you think it will reach my mother's ears?"

"I don't mind what people think."

"But I mind. And our friends. No one visits us anymore."

"They are not so-called friends. My friends care for me."

"While you party with them. I wonder if you really need one of them…"

"Why should I…?"

Why should she? He doesn't answer. It is he who takes care that her life runs smoothly and who puts the best foot forward. It is he who forgives her when he knows others are talking behind his back. He knows the conversation will go nowhere.

"Please!"

She takes her hair together behind her head and rises. "I'm going to sleep."

No promise, no undertaking. He sighs. He will visit his mother and ask her to look after Stefan Friday evening and whether he could sleep over.

He finds the house in George without difficulty. A powerful pickup with mags and wide tyres is standing in the driveway. He peeps into the cabin. Wow, this is really something.

"What are you looking for!" He jerks at the loud voice right behind him.

"Wow! I'm just looking. It is a beautiful pickup. Sorry, I am Petrus Odendaal who made the appointment with you." He puts out his hand.

Pete is a long, solid guy with a darkish complexion, with long black hair tightened in a ponytail behind his head. Not really an attractive guy with a rough appearance. He has an iron grip.

"Oh. All right." Then he looks tenderly at his vehicle. "This is my girlie. No, she isn't just beautiful. She is stunning!"

They laugh and are friends immediately. They walk into his house.

"I drink brandy and Coke. Do you want a drink?"

"Thanks, yea. It was a long drive."

Pet fetches the drinks and glasses. "You want to hear about the accident …"

"Yes. I am doing …" He wants to explain but for Pete any explanation is superfluous. He has told the story dozens of times to all and everyone willing to listen while drinking brandy.

"Look, it was quite a thing. You see it happened like this. That Friday I worked in Oudtshoorn, plumber you know. And we arrived later than I expected and had to rush to get dressed. I wanted to drive to Jeffreys to my girlfriend. Sexy girl. Met her at a dance. There was a party and we were going. So, I had to move my ass."

He swallows a few gulps of his dark drink and sits back in his chair. Ready to tell his big story.

"At Knysna, I had to fill up. When I turned right into the filling station, the green Mercedes passed me and turned in the direction of Jeffreys. I had a quick peep at the driver. Neat, surely a rich fucker, I thought. I filled up. Then I hit the road. I was in a bit of a hurry so I let her run. And she purred like a dream."

Petrus opens his mouth to ask a question but he sees the irritation on Pete's face and shuts his trap. He realizes what is going on. Pete is the hero of this story. What he and his wonderful pickup did is the most important part and not Schoonraad's death. Petrus swallows the last of his drink and pours another one when Pete gestures to the bottle.

"Just short of Plettenberg Bay's turnoff, I saw the green Mercedes far in front of me. Each time we drive around a bend and the road opens up in a straight section, I saw I gained on him. He is travelling quite well but didn't seem in a hurry. And so, I slowly gained on him. Just past Nature's Valley's turnoff, where the road becomes curvy, I was about fifty meters behind him. But when I went around the next bend I saw the guy is racing now. He now is further ahead of me. I thought he had seen me approaching and now wanted to dice me." He laughs with a big open mouth and lifts his glass. He takes a huge gulp.

"Man, then I tickled my baby. And I saw I caught up with him. And I pushed her a little more. We were doing round about hundred and seventy kilometres per hour. Another sharp bend and I saw I was gaining. And I thought this road is up and down with sharp bends. I would keep on his heels. Way ahead the road is more straight and flat then we would see. But then he went over a hillock and is out of sight for a few moments. When I went over, he was halfway down the decline and now he was doing at least one-eighty or more. Ahead I know was the very sharp bend to the left. On the right-hand side is the abyss. I think I was about sixty or seventy yards behind him. And when he went into the bend far too fast I saw there goes the right back tyre. At that speed, he didn't stand a chance. I only saw the smoke of the tyres as he tried to brake, but he swerved over the road and went through the barricade and I saw how the car travelled through the air and then vanish as it begin to tumble. It was like a film, you know. When I stopped, I heard the bump and ran to the edge. I heard the explosion and when I looked down, I saw the car was in flames. A goner. Poor guy."

He pours another drink and sits back. The exhilaration of the narration now passed.

"Wow! It was a horrible experience."

"You can say that again. Never has anything like this happened to me."

They nurture their drinks for a while.

"The newspaper said you had seen something like a whiff of smoke when the tyre burst."

"Yes, this was quite strange. I always thought a tyre bursts and that's that. I could swear it looked like when a bomb cracker exploded. But everything happened so quickly, I could have imagined it."

"And the guy in the white BMW?"

"I don't know if it is important. I even haven't mentioned it to the police. I think I told the reporter about it."

"Where was he?"

"Man, I reckon a fifty yards from the start of the bend. On the right-hand side is a resting place with a tree and a table. He sat there in his car nose pointing to Plettenberg Bay."

"Could you see who was inside?"

"Not really. My eyes were fixed on the Mercedes. We were travelling at a hell of a speed. But after I had stopped and looked over the abyss, I could see he departed in a cloud of dust. That's all."

"So, you think he must have seen the accident? Do you think he was in a terrible hurry to get away?"

"Well, maybe. As I said, his car was pointing in the direction of Knysna. Hang man, the Mercedes' tyres yelled but I don't think he could hear the explosion. He was about over the hill by that time. Maybe he could see in his mirror something went wrong. But you know how it is these days. People don't want to be involved."

"You were the only witness?"

Petrus can see the questions irritate him.

"Yes, the first car that came along from Jeffreys was about five minutes later The driver promised to phone the police with their cellphone. I was late already and drove off."

"Now, what is the top speed of your pickup?"

Pete's face lights up. They chat for another half an hour. Then Petrus goes to his hotel.

He didn't know it was really such a distance. On his way back, he tried Van Zyl's number a few times. When he reached the exchange, they told him the phones would be disconnected for a week. Telkom is working on it.

He phones Karin and tells her he will be away for another few days. It is too far to go home and then drive to the Kalahari. She isn't impressed. It is Friday and he knows she is struggling with the party she will miss.

"Tell Stefan I miss him." She puts the telephone down in his ear. He will have to decide on his mismarriage, he thinks with pain in his heart.

With a map, he plans the shortest route from Knysna to Fisher's Post. While his car follows the two light beams in the road that evening, he has a lot of time to think.

If his visit to Van Zyl is futile, he would have spent a lot of time and money. What does he want to prove, he asks himself? That he still can do proper detective work? That he is trying to correct a blunder from eight years back? And then, he must get clarity about his marriage. Maybe subconsciously, he wants to get distance between him and Karin to get some perspective. He sleeps over in a town in the Karoo. Early the next morning, he is deep into the Kalahari.

Later he leaves the main road and drives on a gravel road to Fisher's Post. White dunes, red dunes, flat dunes with dry bushes like stubble beard motionless in the early sun. Sand under the wheels, sand at the side of the road and dust. Dust clouds that swirl behind his car, follow him for a while and then spread out on both sides hanging there seemingly lazy to get down. He wonders how long it will take for the dust to settle.

Well, the dust didn't settle soon after the bank robbery. After Hannes was taken into custody, the newspapers had a sensational story. All the money was gone and Hannes was somehow portrayed as a lone hero. The robbery was so cleverly planned. The bank wouldn't comment on the millions that have been lost. The robbery was compared to the great bank robberies worldwide. Journalists enjoyed the sensation and came up with saucy stories. Another hot topic was the speculation whether it was a one-man job and if two weeks were enough time to break through the walls.

Two-o'-clock that afternoon he stops in front of the house of Land's End.

Van Zyl suspiciously invites him inside.

He works for a magazine and they are busy with stories about big bank robberies in South Africa. Van Zyl had been working at the bank when a bank robbery took place. He knows it is a long time back, but can they talk about it? No money has ever been found. He rabbles on to put Van Zyl at ease. Maybe the years that have gone by, gave Van Zyl a specific perspective of what had happened.

They sit down in the sitting room. An empty whisky bottle stands on the table.

"I don't know why you bother me after eight years. The thing lies in the past. Only a week ago another guy came who also wanted to talk. Brought a bottle of whisky. I can't even remember what we were talking about. He sells electric equipment or something. He went without showing me his things."

This is a shock for Petrus. He will have to play his cards nicely.

"Oh, I know a few guys doing this," he lies blatantly. "What is his surname, maybe I know him."

Aggressively Van Zyl answers. "If he told me I have forgotten."

"What is he looking like?" Wrong question. He can bite his tongue off.

"Ordinary, with black hair. What is the real reason you are here?"

Van Zyl is mildly sceptic about his story.

"As I have said, we are investigating whether what happened can't be interpreted from a new perspective. As years go by, new and better insights might come to the fore. We are not detectives, we only tell stories and an old story from another viewpoint can be quite interesting even if it solves nothing."

He can see Van Zyl doesn't follow him completely but is more at ease.

"Must be quite lonesome on the farm?" He tries a new strategy.

"Yes, as I have told the guy that was here …"

"Sorry to interrupt. Is he maybe driving a white BMW?" This was a wild guess in the far, desolate, plains of the Kalahari.

"Yes." He was taken by surprise by the question and somewhat confused.

"Okay, I know him well," he says quickly while the blood rushes through his veins. "Yes, he is a hawker. Drives around with his stuff. Nice guy."

"Must say, yes, he is. We had a nice chat." He gestures at the bottle. "With the whisky on top of that." Van Zyl managed to get a dry smile over his lips.

"Now, as I have said to the guy: since my wife's death…"

Van Zyl is now ready to talk but Petrus listens with half an ear. His thoughts are racing with the speed of Pete's pickup. Can this be a coincidence? Is Van Zyl also on Van Velden's list? If it were Van Velden who killed Schoonraad, why is Van Zyl still alive? Or was Hannes only fishing for information? Selling electronic equipment, my goodness! He now has more questions than answers. He is now fairly convinced that Van Velden has started to initiate his threat in the court. Who remains?

Rothwell and himself.

"Where is the car?"

"Parked a few blocks away."

"Are you fucked in your head?" He shakes of inheld fury, white in the face. He holds the newspaper out with the report of Schoonraad's accident.

"What if someone …"

"No one will identify me and no one will identify the car. There are hundreds of white BMWs in the country."

"But only one with that specific number plate. If the guy who saw you got a glimpse of the number plate it can lead to shit."

Smiley is silent for a few moments. He is breathing heavily. Hannes cannot understand why Smiley has summoned him. But then emotion overwhelms Smiley.

"You want Smiley in jail. I told you nicely …"

He has difficulty containing himself. He spills from the drink in his hand on the expensive carpet.

"Where's the key?" He holds out a big, fat hand.

Flabbergasted Hannes hands it over. He gives it to the little man.

"Go get the car. Take it to Mackie's chopshop. Tell him to demolish the car tonight. He must give you the grey Corolla. And move your arse. My heart can't take any more worries."

In the corner at the bar, a bearded man is sitting nurturing his drink. It seems that he has no interest in the happenings in the sitting room. Smiley also hasn't introduced them. The man just sits there and strokes with his finger over his cheek as if there is something he tries to rub away. Smiley gestures to Hannes to sit down.

Jemima in a transparent red blouse and long black trousers gets him a drink.

"How do you know it is me? I mean the newspaper report?"

"Look, if I was fucking stupid, I would have been in jail long ago. I know of everything because I have to know. Jamima, go and make us some hotdogs. I'm famished. The damn Jakkie."

"What about Jakkie?"

"What about Jakkie? What about Jakkie? Jakkie will send my soul to hell, that's what."

So, this is the reason for the superfluous emotion.

"Jakkie disappeared. He was here last night. This morning gone. And why, I ask you, why? He's got everything here. Food, money, and even girls if he wishes. Here is brandy, whisky, beer, you name it, here's everything. But when I turned my back he absconded."

A big teardrop runs over his cheek. He wipes it away with the back of his hand.

"And just now, just before you came, I heard he works for the Greek again."

"For Georgiou? Are you sure?"

Hannes gets an aversive look. Smiley talks loudly. "My men don't lie to me. The last guy who lied to me won't be able to produce children. So, it is the truth and I don't know where my Jakkie is."

Diamonds! Everyone in the underworld knows of Georgiou's unlawful smuggling with diamonds. And everyone knows how shrewd he is. Some of his carriers sit in jail but they never betray him. He stays as clean as a whistle.

"But is he really that stupid?" Hannes is upset and can barely cover his amazement.

"You are all stupid," Smiley screams passionately. "You, Jakkie and the whole fucking lot. Look what you have done!"

He holds out his glass to Jemima who has just put a plate of hotdogs in front of him.

"But it is not the same."

"It may be different but it is the same. You dare too much. And if you are as stupid as Jakkie … The police are after him, he escaped from jail, he was in for murder. His enemies are looking for him. They will slit his throat if they catch him. And now he is working for the Greek!" Smiley throws his arms wide.

"I shall be more careful …"

Smiley says nothing. Peeps at him with pinched eyes over the full glass Jemima has put in his hand.

When he later departs with the Corolla, he is very worried about Jakkie. He suddenly remembers a strange comment from Jakkie: "Smiley has everything, I have fuck-all. When I one day is released I also want something."

A few days later, the police shoots Jakkie after a diamond robbery. Hannes is shocked, Smiley shattered.

"The fucking Greek! Look what he did with my little brother. They say the Greek planned everything very good but he didn't know about a backup security system. The police were on the scene quickly and they ran away. The police fired shots. Jakkie was instantly killed, his mate heavily wounded. And the Greek probably is sitting and laughing his ass off. Everyone knows he is the brain but how do you prove it."

Smiley's big head hangs down and he cries like a baby. After a while, he lifts his head and with tears in his eyes, he says passionately in a hoarse voice: "I swear he will pay for it."

Deep in his heart, Hannes concurs wholeheartedly. They must be brought to book; the rich who misuse others. Most of the time when life turns its back on you, an unscrupulous man sits behind it. Yes, they must pay for their deeds!

The next evening Georgiou is blown to pieces in his Maserati, inside his garage, in his multimillion home.

Rhoode is quite disturbed. When he has reached his home, no one was there. Only a brown envelope on the coffee table in the sitting room. He was amazed but also in a bad mood. He likes things to be perfect. Everything must fit himself. When he saw the photos of him and the girl, Charlotte, he was initially flabbergasted. He must say, these are quite beautiful photos but damning as only photos can be. Instinctively he knows there must be a second set of these because it was done highly professionally. Private detective, thus.

He sits down on the sofa. He must think this through. Firstly, he is amazed that his wife, Clarice, has gotten to such lengths, that she had so much initiative. Their marriage failed a long time ago; they only stay together. It is a case of money, he thinks. He is a rich man and if she leaves him and he is the guilty party, he will have to pay up thousands if not millions. The photos have changed everything. Her sister's husband, his hated brother in law, is an advocate.

Suddenly he boils with frustration. With Clarice, with Charlotte, and himself. Why has Charlotte loitered behind him into the street! The money is the least. He can frustrate them with court appearances for a long time. He can cross-question Clarice in court so that she doesn't come out of it so milky white. But it is his honour, his social position, that will be under scrutiny. Washing dirty laundry in court doesn't fit his status, the newspaper headlines about an unfaithful attorney don't go down well with him. He will have to wait for their next move. He has in any case a lot of hidden money overseas and just maybe he could come off lighter.

He sighs, pours a glass of brandy and enjoys it. Clarice! He can hardly believe it. Always so feeble, so servicing, although the marriage fire between them was long gone. The revenge of a woman, he thinks wryly. He can only hope they will move swiftly so that this thing passes quickly.

What is he going to do the rest of the evening? He rises, takes his jacket. Now that his infidelity is recorded in photos, there is no sense in hiding anything. He doesn't want to stay alone in this big, empty house and Charlotte is a sex-hungry, sexy lady.

Two evenings later his front doorbell rings. He rises to open the door. It is already half dark and he puts on the sitting room's light. A guy with a sort of uniform is standing in front of him.

"Good evening, Mr Rhoodie. I've got a package for you." It irritates the hell out of him if someone calls him Rhoodie instead of Rhoode.

The man's long, black hair shows from under the cap and he wears thick frame goggles with thick lenses. The package is a long stuffed envelope. His name is written in large letters with a koki.

So this is it, Rhoode thinks. They didn't waste any time sending divorce papers.

"Thank you," he says and wants to close the door.

"So sorry, Sir. I must see your ID and you will have to sign for the package." He looks down at a list on a file in his hand. "Can I quickly come in and we'll handle this quickly, please?"

Despondently Rhoode lets him in and gestures to the coffee table. The sooner this irritating guy is gone, the sooner he can have a look at Clarice's documentation. He can even see it in his mind's eye. He gets his ID from his pocket and hands it over. The guy writes down the number.

"One changes a lot during the years," he tries to make a joke but suddenly is Rhoode highly irritated.

"Where must I sign?" he asks brusquely.

The man pushes at his goggles and looks at the list.

"Here, Sir. Here is a pen. Just push the button."

Normally Rhoode likes to sign with his own pen, but now he is in a hurry. He pushes the button at the end and signs hastily. He just glimpses a second at the logo. Blitz Couriers.

He doesn't see the grin on the man's face. He doesn't see how the man strokes his left bearded cheek.

"Thanks," the man says meekly. Then he looks around the room. Beautiful, big sitting room, huge windows with brocade curtains. "Beautiful place. Okay, good night, Sir. Hope you have a pleasant evening."

Rhoode closes the door behind him.

Once outside, he moves to the window. Through the lace curtains, he can see what Rhoode is doing.

"Goodbye, Mr Rhoode. You skunk!"

23 A FOURTH LOOTER?

He rises early on Monday morning. Karin only turns around to sleep on. He walks over to Stefan's room and greets the sleeping child. On the veranda, he picks up the morning newspaper and puts it under his arm. The sun caresses the half-wet leaves after the night's shower with golden rays. On such a day, one must be on a farm somewhere, he thinks. An early morning joy rushes through him. He once again feels Karin's body warm, soft, and willing next to his.

With a smile, he backs out of the garage, stops, and opens the city map and studies his route. He is pleased with himself. Maybe last night was the turning point in their relationship. So near to Karin, he has never felt before. A more exciting day as normal awaits him. The manager of a big production company of specialized electronic equipment is convinced that one of his senior workers smuggles with their equipment. He gets too many complaints from overseas clients of shortages in their deliveries. Sometimes there are empty boxes. They threaten to get another supplier and he must now take drastic action. For him, the obvious person is the senior stock clerk that has the final jurisdiction over the packing and shipping.

Petrus knows from experience, that if the clerk is the guilty party, he will have accomplices. In any case of dishonesty, there is a head, a person who administers the theft. For the next few weeks, he must follow the suspect, find out whom he contacts, and try to put a picture together of what precisely is going on.

In an upbeat neighbourhood in a northern suburb of Johannesburg, he finds the house easily, drive past, turns at the next crossing and stops about fifty yards from the house. On the left, the whole block is a park, with green grass, colourful beds of flowers, and shrubs against a shallow incline. Wonderful! He is quite sure that from the top of the incline you will have a wonderful view over the vicinity and the central business district of Johannesburg. Good! Now his parked vehicle won't attract unnecessary attention. He is only a photographer taking beautiful pictures.

He takes his camera out of its bag, studies it for a while. When he is satisfied that he has the correct lens, he walks up the incline. It is truly an inexpressible sight. His strong lense brings the angular city in the morning light closer to him, the haziness of smog lies like a grey blanket over the city. He takes another photo of the still sleeping city. Then he focusses all around to make sure that he would take excellent photos of the suspect. He has no idea how the man looks.

Exactly seven-o'-clock the man opens his front door. Neatly dressed. Short, black hair, almost parted in the middle of his head. Goggles. Moustache only a thin line. Narrow face. The man moves to his garage. Petrus walks down the decline to his car. The man pulls out and follows the road in the direction of the city centre. He follows him. Nothing suspicious. He drives to his work, go through the security gate and is swallowed by the premises. Petrus parks near the gate and settle in. A long day ahead. According to the manager is it on Mondays that the suspect leaves his office without reason and returns without reason a few hours later.

Petrus gets a file out of his briefcase. He can as well compile the report about the teenager he followed for a long time. The parents were worried that he was involved in Satanism. The reason, however, why he slipped out of the house by night, was far more amorous. His nightly encounters were nothing other than visits to a young, working, sexy brunet.

He has scarcely started when the suspect's car comes through the gate. A few minutes later, he turns into a shopping complex. Petrus parks a few spaces away, puts a cap on his head and goggles. A little disguise can be handy. He follows the man who climbs the stairs to the second storey and follows one of the corridors. Petrus follows stealthily. The man goes through a door that closes behind him. Petrus stops in front of the door. Dr Johan Viljoen, Dentist. Damn! Petrus goes back to his car. An hour later the man emerges, climb into his car and goes back to work.

Petrus sighs when he parks at his vantage point. Well, this is life. He takes the file and writes down the particulars of the teenager's case. Later on, he will type it out, edit it and hand over the printed report to the parents. When he puts it back in the briefcase his eyes fall on the headline in the newspaper: Mystery around attorney's death deepens.

He smiles. Newspapers have also their own way to write their own fiction. He relaxes against the seat and thinks over the different cases he has to investigate. Good planning can eliminate a lot of donkeywork and frustration. And there are several ways to get information about a suspect.

At lunchtime, he becomes hungry. He remembers a stall that is selling hotdogs nearby. It is only a block away and he drives to the stall. A tasty hotdog and a cool drink become a nice lunch.

Back at his post, he lets his thoughts wander. Karin, Stefan, his old mates in the police service. Eventually, he thinks about Hannes van Velden. Well, at this stage he can do nothing.

It is time for the news bulletin. He switches on the radio.

"According to the police, there is no progress in the case of the attorney, Mr Rhoode. Mr Rhoode was injured badly in an explosion on Friday evening. On the way to the hospital in an ambulance, he died. A neighbour who heard the explosion contacted the police. No suspect has been seen at the scene."

Can he believe what he hears? He is flabbergasted. Then he plucks the newspaper from his briefcase and unfolds it. His eyes sweep over the heading. Then he starts reading. His brain has difficulty following the meaning of the words. Rhoode! It can't be! Greedily his eyes devour the contents. The explosion at Rhoode's house. Probably a sort of letter bomb. Mrs Rhoode wasn't at home. No one saw any suspicious movement. Guesswork; an angry client, a jealous mistress? Mrs Rhoode wasn't available for comment.

Mrs Rhoode? A few days ago he sat in front of her with his report. The vengeance of a neglected spouse? He can't believe it. His knowledge of humans tells him that this is not her style. But who knows?

And suddenly the names of the group comes into his mind. Van Velden, Van Zyl, Schoonraad, and Rothwell come together in his confused mind. What did Pete tell him? Something like a bomb cracker exploded from Schoonraad's wheel. The white BMW? And now Rhoode!

In hindsight, he knows he made a terrible mess of his investigation eight years back. He is sure Van Velden is responsible for Schoonraad's death. But Rhoode? Could he be in cahoots with Rothwell and his mates? He defended Hannes at the trial or did he really. A few lame questions in cross-examination to his relief. An excellent lawyer like Rhoode could have smashed Diergaart's testimony. He was afraid it should happen, but it didn't. And it never has bothered him. Now it does.

He switches on his car and drives frantically to the central business district. He must reach Rothwell. Rothwell and himself are the remaining people on Van Velden's list. And anyone can be the first. He phones Jasper. Please get all the information you can about Rhoode. I'm now sure he was also on Van Velden's list. It is a matter of life or death.

While he is still racing, Jaspers phones. "Hell, my boy. This is a terrible mess. Van Velden interested himself in explosives and electronics. He worked at the library and ordered books to study it. He couldn't get enough of it. The guys at the jail were very helpful and said if Jakkie, his great pall, hasn't escaped, they could have talked to him as well."

Now Petrus is quite sure. He parks in the parking garage opposite the building in which Rothwell have an office. He rushes because it is nearly time for the lunch hour and maybe Rothwell can leave for lunch. That said if he is not on vacation or on a business trip. The lift seems to be reluctant to come down. It stops at every floor as the workers come down for their lunch hour. Eventually, he can step inside, but he must stand aside to let a smart man pass. He pushes number 6 hard and long. The lift moves upward. He must orientate himself. Yes, to the right in the longish corridor, around the corner and then one of the doors on the left-hand side. The lift's doors open on the sixth floor.

He is a few yards down the corridor when he hears the loud bang of the explosion.

Rothwell was quite impressed with the businessman with lots of money and many American connections. During their first conversation, the man brought up words like valuta, off-shore investments, fiscal advantages and so on and only said enough to incite him.

"Look, I find our conversation quite beneficial but I must make haste. I have to catch a plane to Hong Kong where a new economic explosion is anticipated and where I want to invest heavily. Everything is explained in this leather-bound file. I will be glad before my departure, even if it is only in principle, to know if you want to take part in my venture."

Rothwell promised to have a look at it as soon as he had finished signing all the letters that urgently had to go out even if it is over lunchtime. The man put down the thick file on Rothwell's desk. Rothwell pulled it closer and his hand caressed the fine leather. His eyes were eagerly shining.

The man rose. "Then I greet you, Mr Rothwell. Rest assured that this meeting has given me much pleasure. I promise you the file will blow your mind."

Hy pressed Rothwell's outstretched hand and left closing the door behind him. He also closed the secretary's door when he stepped into the corridor. He slowly walked down the long corridor.

***

"Shit!!" The explosives expert stares in disbelief at the scene in front of him. "This was a neat job."

He whistles through his teeth while he adorns his plastic gloves and shakes his head.

"Look, not even a window has broken. Just the guy's chest torn to shreds."

The detective with him shivers and tries not to look at the body in front of him. Luckily it is not his work. He has seen hundreds of dead people but this one makes him sick.

"Now let's find out what triggered this explosion." The expert starts to go through everything systematically. Now and then, he lifts something with his tweezer and put it in a plastic bag. With that, he will have scientifically to reconstruct what the bomb was made of, what triggered it and what exactly the impact of the explosion was. He must explain why the whole office wasn't destroyed, but only the man behind his desk was mutilated. A sort of letter bomb, was his first guess, while he gathered pieces of a leather file and put them in his bag. Then he gathers dust on the desk, studies it for any solid pieces of material and puts it in another plastic bag.

"Shit," he says again, "this guy knew what he was doing. He knows his explosives. An artist, that is what he is … It reminds me of…"

"Shut up now, man," the detective says, "I'm trying to concentrate and get a picture. Say the guy shot him with something. As you've said: the office is intact. Even the desk isn't damaged severely. And the explosion didn't ignite a fire."

"Yes, my mate. That's what I also say: it was a neat job. Precise charge probably hid in a file. Triggered probably with the opening of the file but he could have used a remote."

"That would ensure the bomb goes off when the killer plans it," the detective muses.

"That's right. But I'm finished here. Forensics must now take over. Maybe they can find something I missed. You know like hair, tracks or something that can lead one to the killer. I'm going now."

"Okay. See you later. I want to have another word with the secretary. The guy who came in just before lunchtime probably left the thing here. She can't remember much of the guy, only that he was dressed neatly and looked like a stinking rich bugger. Expensive clothing and shoes. Black hair, moustache, beard, attractive. Oh, with goggles. Seemingly an old friend of Rothwell."

He finds her behind her desk.

"I won't take long. Are you feeling better? I know it must have been a harrowing experience and you are still shocked. But somehow one remembers things better. Please again tell me what happened just before lunchtime."

She was about to leave when he came in. Smart, she thought, a rich man. Those clothes and the handkerchief in the pocket, golden framed goggles, ostrich leather shoes. This guy has it! Just arrive from America from his American business deals. He must urgently speak to Rothwell. It can't wait and it is a question of millions. By the way, we are old friends and we've made each other rich. He knows it is lunchtime and she can leave. He and Rottie will discuss it over lunch.

She told Mr Rothwell she is going to lunch but an important man wants to see him urgently. It wasn't strange. Many times people came and discussed business with him over lunchtime. So, she left. The man nodded at her and waved with his hand smiling. She noticed the leather-bound thick file in his hand when she left.

Okay, nothing new and little one can do with for now. He knows that is the best that he will get out of the secretary for now.

"If there is anything else you think is important later on, how trivial it would seem to you, please contact me! I think you must take off for the rest of the day."

They leave the office together. He pulls the door shut behind them. He reads the name in golden letters on the door: H Rothwell, Financial Broker.

He lies on his bed with a fiery longing for Sylvia. After the tension of the past days, he longs for her soft touch, the smell of her hair, their warm cuddling. Wow! It was touch and go. Who would have guessed that Odendaal would gallantly hold the lift's door open for him? He hasn't changed much during eight years. It was the same face that greeted him that morning, only it seemed there was haste in his eyes at the lift. Not the look of winning and triumph. Of course, he had made a mess of the case. There was enough reason to believe that he was made the scapegoat as even more than one reporter mentioned in the newspapers. But what could he say? When no one else was apprehended?

His silence in court was also due to the guy who was locked up in the same cell.

"What for?"

"They say I robbed a bank."

The guy whistled."Yes, I heard the boys talk about it in the bar. My fuck! It was a neat job. I hope you hid the money well where the fuckers can't get it."

"What do you mean?"

"Listen, I'm just talking. Here I sit because my nephew thinks I stole his wife's diamond ring. But I haven't and they can't prove it, but even if I had, I would have stacked it away where no one can find it. If they find a place where you could have been, it's tickets with you. I know, it's not my first time in this fucking place. Was in jail too."

He moved closer confidentially.

"Don't say anything. No explanation, even if they ask you whatever. Keep to your story. You know nothing. Even if they give you an attorney. And if you had pals, don't split on them. The less they know, the weaker is their case and how lighter the sentence. And … the guys in jail don't like splitters."

His last words came to Hannes as a shock. Jailtime wasn't part of his thinking. He hasn't even worried much about laws and courts. He has always walked the straight path. He suddenly realized in what mess Rothwell had landed him. What if he lost his freedom and had to spend time in jail? He began to hate Rothwell with excessive hate.

The guy's words ran like a refrain through his brain. Don't split on your mates! And he knew it wouldn't help him much. To tell the detectives he was forced by Rothwell. They wouldn't believe it and Rothwell would laugh it off.

He decided to remain quiet. He would remain quiet for his small share of the loot. But then already he decided to take revenge on Rothwell and his co-conspirators one day. He would be the judge and the executor. And he will do it also for all the guys that were bedevilled by Rothwell & Co.

Suddenly he thinks about Rachel. Poor Rachel. One day he sat in the same restaurant where they previously had met with the crowd of lunch eaters around him. He sat at a table, but some stood in a long row for takeaways, some sat on stools at a counter divulging hotdogs and chips. Suddenly she was there with hanging shoulders and somewhat unkempt. He called her.

"What the hell is going on with you? I thought you are sitting with the boss' son in Paris or Athens or somewhere."

She almost fell down in a chair opposite him.

"What the hell?" She looked at him intensely. "You don't look too bad. When have I last seen you?"

"Maybe eight years ago. How are you doing?"

"How does it look?"

"Well, when I last saw you, you were a princess ready to catch the prince. What happened?"

"The usual," she sighed. "Just when I had him accustomed to my body and deeply in love with me, his dad intervened. He had chosen the ideal wife for his son. His one business partner's daughter just finished her university degree and was back from an overseas tour. I saw her; she was at the office a few times. An uninteresting, giggling girl. He tried to explain about mutual business interests, about background – my ass - and what else. We could go on seeing each other, he said. I stripped completely. Who the devil did he think I am? A whore? I could have kicked him in the balls. I resigned, and lately, work where I get the best salary, but I hate every moment."

"You mustn't let that put you down. Remember, we promised each other that the fuckers won't win. No one would like to have you as a girlfriend if you look like this and portray such a sullen mood. You look like a loser."

"It is easy for you to talk. Look at your nice suit. Maybe already stinking rich. I remember you had high hopes for the future. Come on, what treasure did you unearth?"

"Eight years in jail."

Her eyes and lips suddenly laughed. "You're joking!"

"It is true."

"Really?"

"Do you remember the big bank heist eight years ago?

"But how could you?"

"Long story. I was framed but that is not what matters now. What matters now is that you won't be a loser."

"I wish I could …"

"You can!"

"Wait, I must go. I try at least to be a good, punctual secretary."

"Give me your address. I shall come by this evening."

When he arrived at her place that evening, he was quite relaxed. He brought an expensive bottle of wine. He longed to be with Sylvia but he knew he should stay away. That was the first place they would look for him. Luckily, Sylvia is ignorant about his whereabouts.

"Wow! You look happy tonight." She was elated to see him.

"Jip. Had a successful mission today. I'm quite happy."

"Tell."

"Forget about it. Only that I think it was a lucky break."

"I wish I could have a lucky break. I've been wondering how I can hit a guy like him like a boxer to the ground."

"That's the wrong attitude. Forget about him. You can't always win the fight. Don't sulk about it. Show them. In the long run, you must win. But let's make something to eat. I am famished. What do you have?"

While they were preparing dinner and drinking the wine, he felt that she was yearning for something. She felt down in the dumps about her unfulfilled dreams. After the meal, they sat with coffee on the sofa. She suddenly put down her cup and shifts nearer to him Then she puts her arms around his neck and kissed him.

"Thanks for visiting me. I think I have courage again. You know, I really loved him, it was not for the money. I have been visited by quite a few other guys since that time, but it is different. With him, I could have shared a life."

He felt sorry for her and stroked her hair. Her soft presence ignited an old desire. He felt her affection and pulled her closer. She turned her head and opened her lips anticipating a kiss. He kissed her softly. She put her arm around his neck and kissed him passionately. Like that day years ago in a beggarly room, the exhilaration of yearning bodies run through them. But then Sylvia's image spoilt the moment.

"Rachel," he said softly.

"It's okay. There is someone else. I can feel it. I understand. Just hold me tightly for a while." That night he slept on her couch. Early in the morning, he hugged her. Maybe they would never see each other again. Good luck!

Now a new life with Sylvia lies ahead. Smiley is already busy with all the necessary documentation. The money he will deposit in different accounts not to attract any attention.

***

The little man is in front of him when he steps out of the restaurant after a quick lunch.

"Smiley says Odendaal is looking for you."

"How does he know?"

"The world is full of other ears ..."

"But I've nothing to do with ..."

"Smiley says you are not the only one who has been fucked by them." He pulls up his shoulders and vanishes in the crowd on the pavement.

Smiley wouldn't have warned him if it wasn't serious. He will have to be even more careful. If the little man can get to him so easily, maybe Petrus Odendaal can also.

26 THE NEXT TARGET?

Petrus races down the streets on his way home. Deep in him bubbles an emotion he can't exactly describe. It feels as if someone has pulled a ladder from under him. Like a decline, he is falling and can't control his fall. Or like a hole in which he is tumbling. Unsurity, fear; he doesn't know. All that he knows is that Karin and Stefan must leave the city.

Schoonraad, Rhoode, Rothwell, days from one another. Van Zyl? He can't complete the whole picture. But he can't take chances. He is sure he is the following on the list. Where? When? How? He is afraid because his enemy is invisible. Instead of him being the hunter, he is now being the hunted. Letter bomb, car bomb, house bomb? He shudders at the thought that something can happen to Stefan and Karin.

Karin and Stefan are at home when he arrived.

"What utter nonsense is this?" Karin is annoyed.

"It is a case of life and death. There is no other choice."

Even after more background, she stays obstinate.

"You and Stefan are going to your parents in the country. I shall explain to your boss. He will understand."

"But can't we depart tomorrow morning?"

He understands immediately. It is Friday evening. The weekly dance. He is silent for a few moments.

"No, you are going to depart now. And …"

Now he must say what he couldn't say for years.

"… if your parties are more important than Stefan and I, you needn't come back. When all is over here, I will come and fetch Stefan. Your choice!"

She opens her mouth to bury him under an avalanche of scathing words, but he holds up his hand.

"This is final! I don't want to hear anything. For the sake of Stefan, yourself, and our wedding, you will have to choose. And now you must go and pack so that you can go. It is about four hour's drive. You can reach there before dark. I am going to phone your parents now. And if you don't go, I will ask my mother to take Stefan."

Furiously she looks at him but then turns around without a word to go and pack. Half an hour later they depart.

Then his phone rings. It is Lucia.

"Ah, my lost cousin. Look, I'm quite happy to be part of your life again, or aren't I?"

"You're making a joke. Maybe not for long. Have you followed the bomb murders?"

"Yes, you know I thrive on sensation. I've just heard about Rothwell. Isn't he one of the names I gave you?"

"He is. I wanted to visit you but things are rough. I think you can start writing your scoop. I visited Van Zyl. Somehow he is still living. But Van Velden had visited him also. With the white BMW that was noticed on the scene of Schoonraad's murder. I didn't know Rhoode was also in the ring, but in any case, he is, or rather was, it seems. He was Rothwell's attorney. I can't join the dots now, but …"

"Could there be other guys as well? Just heard Georgiou was blown to smithereens last night."

"Georgiou, what are you saying? I don't know. Maybe not. He wasn't one of Rottie's pals. But the others, yes. My name is probably on that list also."

"Goodness! And you are so calm. I shudder down my spine. Here is enough stuff for a thriller. Imagine the heading in the newspaper: Detective fears revenge of a bomb murderer, the bank robbery, the names, the murders, the suspect. Will it help to place a photo?"

"You can if you wishes, but I presume he disguises himself very well. I even opened the lift's door for him and didn't recognise him then."

"Where?"

"At Rothwell's building just before the bomb blast."

"Fine. I want all the finest, dirty details."

"Okay. Where can we meet where it is safe?"

"Our restaurant. Security is quite tight here."

"Okay, will visit you later on. Find out whether the police has progressed with one of the murders."

The following days are far worse than a nightmare. The weekend lies like a vast prairie in front of him. He knows he must hunt Van Velden but he has no idea where to start. He tries to go ahead as purposeful as possible. He again visits Sylvia. No go. Systematically he goes through his contacts in the underworld. For them Van Velden is nonexistent. Jasper can't help him. He sits entrapped in the invisible net Van Velden has spun around him. He gets the feeling that he is being watched. An onslaught on his life seems sure. When he drives, he looks in the rear mirror frequently, treats every white BMW with double suspicion. He makes double sure that no one had been in his house when he returns, he sleeps in different rooms at night, only leaves the main bedroom's light on. Gets a security watch to look after the home by day.

While waiting for Jasper, drinking a beer, and seemingly cool and collected, his brain works at the speed of light. The fact that Hannes is invisible, can make his move unexpectedly in any form whatsoever, unnerves him. Hannes seems to play the chameleon. The fact that did not recognise him immediately at the lift, irritates him immensely. He also knows that Hannes won't wait too long. It would be too dangerous for him. The longer he takes, the more leads will point to him and before long the whole police force would be on his trail.

Okay, think like a murderer, is an old saying in the police. But this time it doesn't help. Everything is there. The motive, the method, the victims connected with the bank robbery. But the dots won't join.

He even went as far as to watch Sylvia'shouse clandestinely. Played chameleon himself. Then like an old man, then like a bum loitering past. Watch out of the corner of his eye to see anything suspicious. To no avail. Watched from a distance for any movement nearby through his camera's superlens. Nothing.

Yesterday an unknown car stopped in front of the house. Two occupants. The driver is a lady with black hair. He waited until she left and followed her. Up to a flower shop. Damn!

"You look worse than a scarecrow!" Jasper laughs out loudly. "For how long have you been sitting here?"

"Maybe round about an hour."

"Then you are a real ass. You've almost not touched your beer! No, man. You are acting strangely!"

Petrus smiles. "I am thinking."

Jasper sits down. "Wait, let me order a beer then we can discuss whether your futile thoughts delivered something."

The afternoon lies placidly around them outside the windows. On the dam, ducks swim in a row. Once in a while, one dips underwater looking for food. It fascinates Petrus so intensely that he doesn't hear Jasper's loud voice.

"I solved the case of murder. You helped me a lot last time warning me to not be too hasty."

"Good. I'm glad. I reckon it was the agent, not so?"

"Jip."

"Fill me in." His eyes still are focused on the mother and her ducklings.

"The usual story. Working on his nerves. Visited him up to three times a day. Working on loose ends, I said. And once he diverted from his original alibi. I then hammered him for half an hour on that and then he broke. Sang like a birdie. All the gory details. It was as if it was a relief for him. His nerves were shattered to smithereens." Jasper bursts out laughing. "Maybe I relieved him of manic depression or even suicide."

Their laugh thunders through the room.

"Congratulations, my mate. I'm grateful you hung on. Look at the rubbish I committed and now it is almost overtaking me."

"Don't blame yourself. I would probably have done the same in your shoes. The guys were too clever and that guy … what is his name again?"

"Hannes."

"Yes, Hannes. I feel even sorry for the guy. They messed with him, that Rothwell and his pals. But to blow up the guys one by one is rather excessive."

"Yes, and it helps me zero. I don't get a knife's blade in the oyster to open it. And I walk like the living corps waiting for the dead to happen to me."

"Chase him"

"He is invisible and he is nowhere and he is omnipresent. I even held the lift's door open for him."

"This is serious. Although, somewhere must be something."

"There is no spoor. The police's investigation has stalled. He works utterly professional. He knows explosives, that's the worst of it."

The ducks are again swimming in a long row past his vision. The mother ahead, the ducklings neatly in a row behind her. There is an invisible connection between them. An understanding. A connection, a connection. It whirls through his mind.

"Sorry pal, I didn't hear what you just said."

"Doesn't matter, I can live with your ignorance." He smiles. "But now I want to drink my beer in peace and we can talk about other things. Maybe it will help us later on to get our thoughts on track."

Petrus realize it is only a suggestion to help him out of his dark mood and he appreciates it. They talk about their rugby days, the girls they had courted, the mischief in the police college, and commanders who gave them gas.

It is only two beers later that Jasper looks at his watch.

"Wait. You can't go now. Help me think. The ducks in a row ... sorry you are too shallow to follow ..."

Jasper laughs, shaking his head. "Okay, go on," as he gestures for another beer.

"There is a link, a connection, action follows action, name it what you like, but listen carefully. Hannes comes out of jail. Let's suppose he didn't have a lot of money. Next moment he drives a new, white expensive BMW to the Kalahari."

"Maybe he got hold of the loot he probably hid somewhere."

"Correct, I think, but a week or so later he blew his first victim to hell. He must have laid his hands on electronic equipment and explosives. That he could only obtain in the underworld. I'm sure of that."

Jasper nods. "What has this to do with the ducks?"

Petrus laughs. "Maybe you are not so stupid as you look. Listen now. He comes out of jail. Within days he is organized. You see, the ducks work like this. He had to make contact with someone who has a contact in jail, how I don't know, but the guy outside must be some guy otherwise he wouldn't have gotten accepted and furnished with the right stuff. Guys outside are sceptical about jailbirds. The row works according to my judgement like this. Hannes had a pal in the jail with an influential contact outside that made it possible for Hannes to get everything in an eyewink. Do you follow me? Contact to contact to other contacts. One for the car, another for explosives, another for money, and so on ..."

Jasper takes a huge gulp. "Blimey, who thought of that ... Cute, these little ducks in a row. Now, who is the first duck in the jail."

"You told me it was a guy named Jakkie. The guy that gaffed the oke with a knife at a railway station. The guys in the jail told you they were big mates."

Jasper nods and strokes with his finger down the side of the glass. Then he starts to turn the glass around. Then he lifts the glass and aims through it. Petrus knows that now that brain is working full-steam. If there were peanuts, he would have stuffed them in his mouth one by one without chewing them. Petrus can't help himself to smile at his dear friend.

"Smiley! My hell, Smiley!" His voice thunders through the room and he hits the table with a big fist. The waiter comes running up scared to death. Petrus waves him away.

"Smiley?" He has heard the name somewhere. "Which duck is he?"

"Look," Jasper is leaning forward. "Hannes was Jakkie's pal in jail. Smiley is Jakkie's brother. He is one of the most infamous but clever swindlers in the country. Finger in almost every dirty pie, but as clean as a sterilized baby towel. Yes, yes. It can only be Smiley. He has contacts all over in the underworld."

He gulps down half of his glass of beer in one swallow. Again he hits the table so that Petrus' beer spills. Again the waiter rushes towards them agitated.

"Where does one find Smiley?"

"That's the problem. And it won't help to look for Jakkie. He was found at a burglary and ran away. He was shot to death. We have an address of Smiley, but when we investigated, we found only empty storerooms with a lot of empty boxes. No Smiley. We don't even know how he looks nowadays. Forge everything he can lay his hands on, people tell us. I swear that white BMW of Hannes was given to him by Smiley."

"How does this help me?"

Jasper looks long and silently over his glass to Petrus. "It doesn't help. I can give you the address and then you're on your own."

"Time, I don't have time for a long investigation. I could be a victim every moment."

Pensively Jasper nods. "I will have a look at Smiley's file and let you know if I find something extra. Promise me you will phone me immediately when you come upon something."

He jots the address on a piece of paper coming out of his jacket. "Good luck, but I must go now."

A half an hour later Petrus drives down the street of the address. He follows the numbers more or less. He notices the number skewishly painted on a skew bord. Nothing strange about the little gate in a high wall. Slowly he passes but from the car, he cannot make out much. Only the grim plastered walls with small windows covered with paint. It looks as if the complex consists of a double story of storerooms. He drives around the corner but also here is a high wall with on and off a garage door entrance. Outside there is no movement whatsoever, no sign of any functional storage on the inside. Well, it is a nice place for illegal activities, nicely hidden and inaccessible.

It is time to visit Lucia.

Lucia, as always, is overdelighted to see him.

"You are tense, my darling," she babbles after a wet kiss.

"Well, with reason, I

think." He enlightens her shortly about everything.

"Shame and I like you so much. To whom will I long if you have left this world?"

"You are joking. This thing is serious."

"I know." She suddenly is the mother hen. "With what can I help you?"

"Two things. Write again about the serial killer. Join the murders of Schoonies, Rhoode and Rothwell strongly with the bank robbery eight years ago. Say the police are hot on his heels."

"Are they?"

"Not really. Jasper and his colleagues are also in a spin but he can sleep peacefully. It is my life that is in danger from a bomb or other attack."

"Okay, I will do it. Exaggerate here and there. Hint at the profile of a serial killer. Snub at the so-called rehabilitation of correctional services, and so on. But why?"

"I want to make him nervous. To force him to do maybe a dumb, overhasty thing. I try to give him no chance to set a bomb that I won't uncover. I have enough security in and around my home and special guards to guard my car."

"Wow. And the second thing?"

"You have a friend working at the municipality, not so?"

"Jip, she works at the planning division, house plans, rezoning, that kind of stuff."

"Excellent. I am looking for plans for a specific block of warehouses in Mayfair."

"Why?"

"Will tell you later. Then you put it in a huge scoop."

"You pig. Shall I phone her?"

"If you do it I'll allow you to kiss me again."

"You're two pigs. Give me the address."

An hour later he sits in a restaurant studying the plans. The copies aren't very clear. It seems like old plans. The girl explained that she couldn't guarantee the correctness of the plans, as people could have altered the insides without handing in plans for alterations. They could have constructed walls inside or built new rooms without the municipality's consent. It happens all the time in that old part of the city.

All that he knows is that he must imprint the lines clearly into his mind. Tonight's story will be in the dark. It is not going to be easy. During the day, you can be sure security will be tight. On second thoughts, he decided to go before sunrise tomorrow morning.

He waits until the pitch dark of the night subsides. The faint morning light creeps over the walls and the dark places and where the sun never shines, the grimdark remains. His car he left long before sunrise two blocks away near the railway station. Nothing moves in the street. The faint streetlights that tried to fight the pitch dark are now only glimmering covered by the large trees. Darkness is his mate. The darker the better.

Slowly he walks down the high wall. He plays chameleon. Clad in black, with his collar upright, a cap on his head. Slowly the light wins over the dark. He stops at 62c's dilapidated little gate. Looks quickly down and up the road. He pushes and the gate squeakily opens.

In the dim light, he sees he is in some sort of a small courtyard surrounded by high walls. No passage to any part of the building. This is a cul de sac. He moves out to the street and closes the gate. Well, he was warned about this. He walks along the length of the wall and tries to get the profile of the building paring it with what he learned from the plans.

This is confusing. The high wall runs up to the corner. The light is a little better and suddenly he is at another little gate. There is no bell or handle on the outside but there is a hole in the solid wood scarcely bigger than a man's hand. It must be a second sort of courtyard.

Intuitively he knows that this will give him leeway to reach the building. He smiles. If this is Smiley's hideout, Smiley is shrewd.

He puts his hand through the hole and feels to the left and right. Then he feels it. The bell. His smile becomes wider. Clever to hide the entrance and only one who has been enlightened would know of the bell. He tries to feel if there was a latch to open the gate, but he feels nothing. He can't even think about pressing the bell. It is half-past five in the morning and still dead quiet all around him. Well, if there isn't a latch, he will have to climb over.

A few moments later, he stands before an apparently impenetrable wall overgrown by ivy after he has gone through an iron gate and a narrow corridor. Another cul de sac? He can't believe it.

According to the plan, an entrance should be right in front of him. He switches on his small flashlight and moves through the rubble to the wall in front of him. In the narrow space, he moves along the wall shining his light close to the wall looking for some breach in it.

First, he moves to the left, comes back to the middle and moves right. Nothing.

Can he believe his eyes? Are the plans wrong or so old that alterations made them useless? Moving back, he stumbles against a stack of boxes against the wall. They are empty and the top ones threaten to topple. He gets a mighty fright.

To get the boxes stacked, he has to move the bottom ones away from the wall. And then he sees it. A minute slit in the wall. He pushes the ivy away and follows the slit with his light. It is a door. This is an entrance to the inside. He takes out his pocket-knife and with the blade follows the slit. It becomes stuck halfway up the door. A lock. No handle on the outside. Now he will have to use all his ingenuity and maybe his special apparatus. The dawn is now breaking and sleepers on the inside might now awaken and his advantage of surprise will be gone. He could even be in another cul de sac.

He carefully pushes a thin piece of plastic in the slit where he thinks the lock might be. He is absolutely amazed when the lock clicks softly open and the door opens without a sound to the inside. He kills his light immediately. He is breathing heavily. Is his presence discovered? His heart beats in his chest. For moments, he stands dead still. He listens intently but all is quiet. He relaxes and steps inside closing the door silently behind him

He enters a strange twilight world. The world of Smiley? He can only make out forms of expensive furniture and glass tables and a couch and chairs. He sees a big desk with a laptop with more than one monitor on it. Bottles of liquor in the corner at a bar. When he moves slowly forward, he feels the thick, expensive carpet softly under his feet. A big luxurious room. Can it be or is it a mirage in the middle of the unorderly warehouses?

Suddenly a faint light shines through the opening door in the left wall. He ducks behind the couch, lifts himself to his knees and peeps around the couch. It is an unreal fairy scene. She enters through the door on the left side with only a panty and a thin transparent top, her long black hair a mess falling over her shoulders. She looks down toward the carpet and holds her head with her left hand. She has a terrible headache. She moves past the couch. Her bare feet make no sound on the soft carpet. In the half-dark, she is only a profile moving past him with pointed breasts.

So sudden was her appearance that he doesn't have a plan. He hears her fidgeting amongst the bottles at the bar. Then she bursts out in a string of swear words the equivalent of a sailor's when a bottle topples with a bang. Her voice is hoarse and shivery. He reckons she is still under the influence of drugs or whatever. Then he chooses a strategy.

He moves to the desk and switches on the table lamp on it. Stunned she turns around and the glass of liquor she has just poured shoots through the air. It drops down on the floor without a noise.

"Shit! Fuck! Hell!" she cries white of shock. Then she suddenly gets life and tries to run past him to the door through which she has entered, but he catches her on the arm and presses her down on the couch. In the light, he can observe her better. Dark eyes that see nothing and heavy bags under her eyes. She is gasping for breath. Eyes afraid and shocked.

"What do you use? LSD, Tik, coke? Just tell me. You are in big problems. Do you know how many years you spend in jail for his type of thing?"

His unfriendly voice gets her to widen her eyes and she licks over her dry lips. She begins to wail softly.

"Listen to me carefully. I'm looking for Smiley."

"He's not here."

Sharp! Then this is Smiley's place.

Her voice is dark and hoarse and she speaks like some drunk.

"I'm telling you again. You are in big trouble, my girl, and I think you lie to me."

"I don't lie. He is in Durban."

"From when …?"

"I don't know. I've been alone for a few days."

"And his helpers?"

"There is …"

It is as if her confused mind tells her that she has said too much.

"You must speak up now. If you help me, I will help you, otherwise …"

The threat lets her spill the beans quickly.

Smiley is in Durban, she doesn't know why and what he does. The only helper Smiley allow near him is a short man, and now and then strangers visit Smiley. While she speaks, he is amazed at the beauty of the girl. Maybe not even eighteen years of age and he feels sorry for her. The dull eyes and the bags underneath them tell him that she is extremely addicted to alcohol and maybe different kinds of drugs. What can the future be for a kid like this? Maybe abducted from even more desperate circumstances and promised heaven only to become a drug and sex slave. How filthy can human beings be? But now he needs her.

"Tell me about Hannes, Jakkie's jail pal."

"He was here a few times. I don't know everything. Smiley helped him with cars and so on …"

"When last was he here?"

"I don't know," she tries to avoid answering, but his demanding posture forces her to speak. "Yesterday … the day before. Hell, I don't know. I have a hell of a headache. Smiley gave him another car."

"What else?"

"Shit! How must I know? An envelope with maybe passports and IDs. I fucking don't know. And a little box, I think."

"With what in it?"

"I don't know. I know nothing." She starts crying.

"Could it be a weapon?"

"Maybe. It was wrapped in a cloth or paper and I was on my way out because Smiley said I should fuck off."

She sniffs violently and wrings her hands together and asks nervously. "Can I now get a drink, please? I'm finished."

He takes her by the arm. "Your days of drinks are over, my girl. Come, go and pack a few things and go with me."

He looks up and is shocked. Smiley has entered through the door behind the desk silently and aims his revolver at him. His lifeless eyes tell only one thing: it is either you or I. It is only the couch and five meters that separate them. For a second the earth stands still.

Petrus pushes Jemima violently away as he dives down to the floor. Smiley's lead misses him by centimetres and shatters a beautiful porcelain statuette on a table near the bar. Smiley utters a loud string of swears. Petrus rolls to the right in the hope to get Smiley in his aim but is unsuccessful. He decides on the second-best thing. He targets the massive crystal chandelier hanging more or less over Smiley's head. Maybe he will be lucky to shoot the chain off and then the whole thing will be tumbling down on Smiley. But it doesn't happen. He shoots off one of the cables and a lot of crystals come raining down on Smiley. Smiley swears out loudly again and shoots two rounds into the couch probably hoping to shoot through it and hit Petrus but he is rolling further and then suddenly he sees Smiley partially, creeping on all fours to the back of the couch.

"Okay, my big man. Let go of that shooting iron of yours or I'll blow your head off. Now!"

Smiley glimpses toward Petrus. The gun is aiming straight at his head. His gun is in his right hand on the floor. He lets go of his pistol and slowly rises with his hands up in the air. He looks at Petrus with big eyes. Then, suddenly he grabs his chest. The exhilaration was too much for his overweight body and the small heart within. He falls down unconscious and hits the carpet with a soft thud.

Ten minutes later the medics carry his body out to an ambulance.

Petrus phones Jasper. "I've got a little present for you."

Jemima placidly follows Petrus. Alcohol, drugs, headache, wild west shooting so early in the morning is unnerving. Half an hour later, he drops Jemima off at Sister Els at the centrum for addicted juveniles. He hopes for a better life for her.

So, maybe not a bomb but a bullet in his body. So sorry he couldn't have a chat with Smiley. And not even for a day or two according to the medics. It was a severe heart attack. Hannes probably decided to change his strategy because of his watertight security. But it doesn't mean this is less dangerous. Maybe it could be even more dangerous. If the thing in the package was a gun of some sort, he has to be even more vigilant.

On the way to his home, he suddenly realised that he is hungry. Luckily, there is a supermarket close to his home. He yawns. Well, a nice nap is what he needs now. He turns into the supermarket's parking area. A black Jetta turns in moments later in and the driver parks his car away from the others.

The old man moves slowly with his shopping bag at the backside of the parked vehicles. Then he moves in between two parked cars. For a moment, he stands dead still. Then he takes a smaller bag out of his shopping bag. Quickly he looks around. Then slowly he bends. When he becomes erect, he has only the empty shopping bag in his hand. Slowly he walks back to the black Jetta, switches the car on and starts to drive slowly forward.

Petrus exits the shop just in time to see the old man putting his shopping bag in the Jetta. He is suspicious immediately. There are not many cars this early in the parking area and the black Jetta wasn't there when he went into the shop. Quickly he taps his memory. He hasn't seen the old bloke in the shop. Not even when he walked to the shop. Also not at the pay points. He was in there for just a minute or so to buy milk and bread. Where has this man so suddenly bought his stuff?

He tries to walk as calmly as possible to his car. Out of the corner of his eye, he tries to follow the Jetta but a delivery van moves in between them. He runs to his car. He looks for the Jetta and sees it turning out of the parking area into the street.

He throws his shopping bag in his car and bends down on his knees. He expects the explosives would have been attached to the chassis magnetically near the driver's seat. Cold sweat forms on his forehead. The thing may explode any second. Then he feels it. Square and smooth. He plucks at it and it comes loose.

Amazed he looks at the little black box. Neat piece of work.

But then he quickly gets into action. He must in seconds disconnect the mechanism that could be triggered by a remote. His fingers are clumsy at first. His body burns as if it has an uncontrollable fever. Then he forces himself to be calm. He disengages the lid. Meticulously he follows the wires until he is sure he has the right one. He hesitates for a second. If it is the wrong wire he would be blown to pieces. He plucks hard on the wire, The wire comes loose. The bomb is harmless.

While he is driving home, calmness sweeps over him. He is now sure he is the next target. For the first time, his follower has shown himself. For the first time, the initiative has slightly shifted. His bomb is harmless. He knows now that Hannes drives a black Jetta. That's probably the car he picked up at Smiley, according to Jemima. And he wouldn't know that the bomb has been deactivated. When Hannes pushes the button he will wonder where he slipped up, why the bomb doesn't work. For a moment, Petrus wonders how it would feel to be blasted to eternity. Shock, flames, over thundering noise? He shrugs.

A few blocks further, he sees in the mirror how a black Jetta turns into the street behind him. Could it be the same Jetta? How many black Jettas are there in Johannesburg?

His cellphone rings.

"Hello."

Silence.

"Hello. Petrus Odendaal speaking."

Silence.

Suddenly a light shoots through his brain. The bomb is supposed to explode with the ring of his phone.

"Hannes, if it is you, forget about it. Your little plaything is harmless. I know something about bombs. I know you are quite near me." He struggles to get to the right words to utter. "Speak to me." He waits a few seconds. Then hears a burst of loud laughter. The connection is severed.

Silence. He talks quickly.

"I've been at Smiley. I know everything about you. I'm hot on your heels. Leave your tricks and hand yourself over. Remember it is now me or you. Only one is going to live. And it could be me. Don't seek your death."

Then he realises that he speaks to a dead phone.

At home, he quickly eats a slice of bread, down a cup of coffee and hastens to his car. He will first take the bomb to Jasper and his guys, then he will go to Lucia to fill her in. He is in debt with her and if he doesn't survive …

On his way, he takes a detour and passes Sylvia's house. If Hannes follows him, the fact that he spies on Sylvia would make him more nervous. And this thing must be driven to an outcome. His own nerves are not shatterproof.

He spends the rest of the morning at the detectives and the bomb squad and lunchtime, he and Jaspers visit their old spot for a quick beer. He arrives at Lucia much later than he had planned.

"Sis, you smell of beer. Nice if you don't work and can go to the bar anytime you want. It's like a holiday."

"With an unseen murderer on your heels, it is no joke."

"My poor cousin. Come sit. Tell me everything."

"Okay, I'll tell you everything. I think the climax isn't far off. If I don't survive I would have liked to get the whole picture in writing. Also for the sake of Karin and the little innocent Stefan."

Dusk has set in when he drops Lucia at her home. The city of Johannesburg is covered with a blanket of smog. A dark, grizzly night lies ahead.

On his way home, he wonders whether he is doing the right thing. Should he not stay away from his home? Frequently he looks in the rear mirror, but there are too may cars and lights to see something suspicious. He can't shrug off the feeling that disaster is following him. Near his home, he imagines someone is following him, but then the lights vanish. Was the car black? He shivers. If it is Hannes …

At his home, he parks the car quickly in the garage, goes in at the back door, inspects the whole home, even looks at the hair he spanned at the front door. Then he gathers some edibles, switches off all the lights except the faint bedlamp in the main bedroom. He locks the back door, turns the key parallel in the lock and put a broom under the handle. He checks the front door. Eventually, he sits down in the recliner in the sitting room. He is in a postion that he can see the staircase going up to the second storey. He switches off the table lamp on the coffeetable next to him. The corridor in front of the bedrooms is in gray twilight. A long night awaits him. Slowly he starts to nibble on one of his sandwiches.

In his hotelroom, Hannes is putting together all his stuff. He smiles. What did Smiley say about leaving tracks? He must make sure he leaves no spoor or soon the police force will be on his trail. He is sure that after Schoonraad's accident, Rhoode and Rothwell's demise they are looking for him. But today he did a great thing. He and Sylvia must only get over the border safely with most of his money. In Botswana, a new future winks at them. He smiles wryly. He hopes he will be more successful than Van Zyl.

On his way back from Van Zyl he thought deeply also about his years in jail.

He knows now that he took the right decision. He only hopes things will run smoothly from now on. He and Sylvia can build a beautiful future. Most of his money are in different accounts. Smiley made sure they have the correct documentation so that he won't easily be stopped at the border.

He puts another document carefully in his briefcase. It is a contract and the door to his future. For that reason, he had to drive all the way to George. The directors who wanted to see him were attending a golfbreak. They have a big building project in Botswana. They offered him a contract. With the contract on the seat next to him, he drove for quite a while, turned back and then stopped at a resting place to study it. Years ago, he was ensnared by a contract. Not again. He studied it intensively. No snags and even in plain English. They would meet him at the golfclub late in the afternoon. Suddenly he realised that he should be going to be in time for the appointment precisely at six. All the directors woud be there but only for a short while.

He was satisfied with the contract. He put it on the seat. He heard a car racing past in the opposite direction. He moved slowly forward. Then a black cab raced by. He shook his head. Well, time is running out.

As many times in the past, he misjudged the power of the BMW. The wheels spun in the loose gravel and kicked up a lot of dust. Then threy gripped and he shot forward kicking dust up until he reached the tarmac. In his rear mirror, he imagined seeing the red brake lights of the pickup. Maybe something happened. He didn't know how sharp the bend was. But then he was over the first hillock and could see nothing more.

He is now smiling as he thinks how he suddenly saw Odendaal face to face. He had to collect extra documentation at the head office in Rothwell's building.

The little man suddenly opens his door. He is in a teribble hurry. Smiley has gone to Durban and he must look after everything. He needs the car. A little later, he drops Hannes a few blocks form Sylvia's home. Without greeting, he races away. Oh, well. In the meantime, they will have to use Sylvia's car.

***

The hangman stood dead still after Smiley went trough the door. Still in the dark, he could see through a small opening of the almost closed door what was happening inside. He could do nothing. His weapon was in the Jetta. Unbelievable! Smiley had misjudged Odendaal. He and Smiley were in a fix. He wanted to plan everything meticulously just as he had done with Schoonraad, Rhoode and Rothwell, but after Jakkie's death, Smiley's nerves were in shreds.

"Odendaal is going to catch Hannes. He is going to lead the police to us. Our days are numbered. Hell man, either leave Odendaal or make a plan quickly."

When he saw Smiley go down, he stepped back slowly, walked back through the rubble to the garage. He hid there until he heard the sirens of the police vans. Then he jumped into the Jetta. Near the station, he saw Odendaal's parked car. He stopped and waited.

Odendaal, he promised himself. Before sunrise tomorrow, you are a corpse.

***

He must have dozed off by ten-o'-clock. Something must have awakened him. It is half past eleven. He listens intently. It is dead quite. Then he realises what awakened him. A faint crack of one of the wooden steps of the staircase. He freezes in his chair. Then he becomes aware of the figure that scarcely five meters from him, is slowly ascending the staircase. The faint light from the bedroom is too little to make it out clearly. He follows the figures with his senses. He holds up his breath. Slowly his hand grips the revolver that lies on the armrest of the chair.

Seconds seem like enternities. Every sinew in his body is tense. Only when the figure reaches the top of the stairs he can make out a dull form. Calmness washes over him like a big wave. Eventually, the invisible becomes visible and touchable. He also knows that he has the initiative. Only the barrel of his gun follows the killer. For the rest he sits dead still.

At the top of the stairs, the figure halts. He looks around in the dark. Everything is dark and quiet. He smiles when he sees the open bedroom door with the dull light shining from the bedlamp. Final settlement. Tomorrow he will be on his way overseas. His hand grips his pistol tighter. Slowly he moves to the bedroom door through which a dim light shines.

Petrus watches as the figure becomes more clear nearer to the door. An easy target now. His finger itches to pull the trigger, but then the figure moves quickly through the door opening. Three times the pistol coughs through a muffler. Petrus smiles. He knows that the pillows he arranged in the form of a sleeping man under the duvet have been shattered.

Almost too soon, he appears in the door opening, now clearly silhouetted against the light behind him.

"Let your weapon fall, Hannes. You are under arrest. Don't try …"

Over hastily the man shoots in the direction where he reckons the voice comes from. The table lamp is shot to pieces.

"Let go of your weapon or I …"

The next shot hits the armrest of the chair. Petrus has no choice. He pulls the trigger.

The figure spins around. He flees into the room. Moments later the solid windowpane of the window is shattered. When Petrus reaches the backyard, there is no one in sight. He must have gone over the back fence. Quickly he phones the police. He gets a strong flashlight and tries to figure out in which direction Hannes escaped. Blood spots runs to the fence at the back. He tries to peep over but the yard is overgrown with bushes. If he is hiding next door, it is too dangerous to follow him. In the distance, he can hear the sirens of the police.

With their flash-lights, they ascertain that he didn't jump over the back fence. The blood spots runs along the fence to the corner where he climbed over into the neighbour's garden.

After searching the area thoroughly they find in the street a smal pool of blood. But then nothing further.

"He must have climbed into his car here," the policeman says. "He is not too seriously wounded. There is not so much blood."

"I reckon I have wounded him in the stomach or hip. I didn't want to aim too high. But it can be that I missed him altogether. Maybe the glass cut him."

"Let's check it out."

The policeman takes out his walkie-talkie. Petrus walks to his home. When he checks the study, he sees a window pane neatly taken out next to the lock of the sliding door. So, that's how he entered. Very clever.

He sits down in the chair. A constable comes in with a duvet.

Petrus jumps up. He phones Jasper. When he arrived at Sylvia's home, two constables are waiting for him.

"Jasper says he is on his way. It will take some time. We musn't wait for him."

"Are you ready?" They nod. They approach the front door. Light in the sitting room is on. He is satisfied that his hunch is the correct one. A wounded Hannes would only choose one place to run to quickly.

On the veranda, he quickly checks on the constables. With their guns in their hands, they are ready. He knocks on the door.

For a few moments, there is silence. He knocks again. Then he can make out through the smoked glass, a figure coming to the door. The door opens. Hannes stands in a gown in front of him.

For moments, they stare speechless at each other.

Eventually, Petrus gets his voice back. "Hannes van Velden. This time I've got you. Where did I shoot you?"

Hannes' mouth falls open. "Shot me?" He is flabbergasted.

"Shot, yes. When you tried to murder me"

"To what? You must be totally insane. When?"

"A short while ago."

"You are more than out of your mind, Odendaal. I haven't put a foot outside this house this evening."

"It won't help to deny it. There were blood spots …"

"So, you shot me. You make me laugh. Don't make the same fault twice. Last time you made a terrible hash of your investigation."

Hannes slowly takes off his gown and stands naked in front of them except for a jockey. He turns around. There is no wound on his whole body. He adorns the gown again.

"Maybe you must let these two dwarfs go. Then you can come in and we can talk."

Petrus nods at them. "Are you sure?" one of them asks.

"Dead sure." They go to their van and drive off.

"I know it is very late. But I got a terrible fright when I saw you in front of me. What about a round of whisky?"

Petrus follows him meekly into the sitting room. His mind is in a whirl. He was wrong second time around. How stupid can one be?

"Only tonight I have learned about Rhoode and Rothwell. So, you think I have blown them all to hell." He gulps his clean whisky. "Let's be honest with each other and then you promise me to leave me alone."

Petrus nods.

"Yes, I educated myself about explosives. When I came out, I had a clear mission to blow them all to hell. Especially Rothwell. He was the brain behind everything and the shrewd attorney his first ally and Schoonraad his bosom cunning pal."

He takes another swig.

"I was at van Zyl …"

"I know. I also visited him. He told me about the guy with the white BMW. The same BMW that was parked near the bend where Schoonraad went over the cliff."

"That was mere coincidence. I was sitting there studying a contract. I know nothing about Schoonraad …"

Petrus gestures that he must continue.

"I just couldn't harm Van Zyl. He was so pathetic and had also been cheated by Rothwell and company. But while I was driving back through the endless plains, I got new perspective. And I thought about what I had. I am a builder, have a sound knowledge of explosives, have some money. I applied for a post at a huge building firm, and above all I had Sylvia. The construction company wants a supervisor over a big project in Botswana. All that was enough to make a new start. If they catch me for murder, I will be in jail for the rest of my life. And jail is no joke. Somewhere along the way, I stopped, destroyed, and buried my electronic equipment and explosives in a deep donga. That was the beginning of my new life. I had to hide because of the money and because you were on my spoor."

There is a soft knock on the door. "It's Jasper, an old colleague. Do you mind if he joins us?"

"No problem. Only if you are going to leave me alone." Petrus nods.

"Then, no problem."

Quickly they sum it up for Jasper.

"Once again it was too easy, not so?" He grins at Petrus.

Hannes looks at them questioningly. "Don't worry. It is just a joke between us … But the question now is …"

"Yes, and the one on which I will be delighted to get an answer. For the second time, I am the pig in the story. The last time completely innocent."

Now the two look questioningly at him.

"Listen let's call a spade a spade. I was complicit in the bank robbery but I was blackmailed." He sketches the whole story shortly. Only he doesn't tell them about the money.

"Then my suspicion that Rotties was a major crook, was correct."

"But who blew up the guys? If you can give us a hint, please do so."

Hannes is quiet for a long while. He is looking sternly forward while thinking deeply.

"With that, I can honestly not help you. But I am going to say one thing. But on one condition."

"Condition?" Jasper asks quickly.

"That you from now on climb off my back. I paid for my infringement. I have been offered a fantastic job in Botswana. Sylvia and I are leaving tomorrow. I don't want to get stopped at the border."

"No problem. We have nothing against you further. Spit it out."

"There was another guy involved in the bank robbery. I didn't know who it was. He was the driver of the van who took them from the scene. I saw him in jail once. He was in for drugs and manslaughter. He did do work for Rothwell. Tried to bomb a safe or something like that. He has a long scar on his face."

"The executioner," Jasper says with a hoarse voice.

"I thought he went overseas."

"Me too. Do you know where he is now?"

"No idea. I saw him once at Smiley. Maybe he could have killed Georgiou as well. I suppose he was done in by Rothwell & Co." He keeps what the little man told him secretly. He didn't understand it then but now it is crystal clear.

Jasper laughs. "Petrus, I know about a place where he frequently hangs out. Let's sort him out."

***

Carl Greeff, alias The Executioner, is gritting his teeth. The bullet went through his side. He will not die but it is extremely sore and bleeding. And he doesn't like blood. He sits in his car, only a few blocks from Odendaal's home. He tore off a piece of his shirt and pressed it down on the bleeding wound hoping it would also help for the pain.

Eventually, the pain subsides. The wound seems to have stopped bleeding. It is time to be calm and make a plan. He doesn't like failures, by Jove, this is the first of his career. He must now concentrate on the next step.

When Van Zyl phoned him, he knew their time had come. Van Zyl yearned for revenge. He himself yearned for revenge. Rothwell and his inner circle had done them in terribly. Van Zyl with a consolation prize and with a threat that they easily could divulge that he was their contact in the bank. He himself wasted a few years in jail after a robbery for Rothwell had gone wiry and when he threatened to spill the beans on the bank robbery, they tried to kill him in jail. If he hadn't been so alert, he could have gotten his throat slit instead of a cut along his face.

Hannes's release was manna from heaven. He knew from inmates Hannes studied explosives and that he promised revenge. He, The Executioner, must do it in Hannes' place. If they would suspect Hannes, one of two things could happen. They could believe his story that he didn't kill anyone and then everyone comes scot-free, or they can disbelieve him … sorry for Hannes.

Schoonraad was easy. Smiley told him Hannes would be in George on that Friday. He knew Schoonraad's moves. A few telephone calls to Schoonraad's house and office, pretending to be a secretary of an important firm that wishes to do business with him, gave him all the information he needed. He knew late on that Friday afternoon, Schoonraad would be driving to Jeffreys Bay.

He tracked Schoonraad easily. It was Tuesday and he had a few days to get his plans nicely together.

On Wednesday, he drove to Jeffreys and found Schoonraad's holiday home. Beautiful against a hillock overlooking the sea. Only a caretaker there. I am an insurance agent. Mr Schoonraad? No, he is at George. Mrs Schoonraad? She's in Johannesburg, only comes on school holidays. Good, I will get him in George. What is your surname? Willemse, thanks a lot, Mr Willemse.

On Friday, he went to the golf course and magnetically fixed the bomb to the back right wheel. And even a tracking device. After lunch, he drove to the sharp bend, hid his vehicle in a clump of bushes. He climbed the hillock above the excavation and hid behind the shrubs and bushes. He switched on his electronic equipment and waited. He could see the whole road from the hill down to the sharp bend beneath him.

Later on, someone in a white BMW arrived, made a u-turn and parked in the shade of a tree. It looks as if he was concentrating on some reading material.

Rhoode was child's play and so Georgiou. But he smiles as he thinks about Rothwell. He is proud of himself. Rothwell's secretary was super punctual. She took her lunch hour precisely at one-o'-clock and precisely an hour later she returned. In the days he watched her, the pattern was fixed even if there were clients. Such predictability helped him to plan wisely.

Even if he only was the driver the evening of the robbery, he expected a good cut. But Rothwell and his pals bedevilled him. With his police record, he would have been the worst off if they were caught and they knew it. For all the work he had done for Rothwell, assaults, bribing, blackmail, motor bombing, they paid him peanuts. And when he threatened to spill the beans, they planted drugs in his room and phoned the police. Even hinted that he was responsible for the injuries of the person when he blew the safe. He got six years for that.

He suddenly realises that he is reliving the past. It is the pain and blood loss. But now he must focus on his present situation.

He scarcely can believe his eyes. The car that slowly drives past in front of him is that of Odendaal. On his way to?

He starts his car and follows slowly. Odendaal still thinks he is Van Velden. When Odendaal turns left and follows the road to the western suburbs, he knows. He smiles. He has shot two rounds in the house. On the third bullet, Odendaal's name is written.

Odendaal still thinks it is Hannes who killed the guys. It was exactly what his old friend, Van Zyl, predicted. Odendaal surely must believe he'll find the wounded guy at Sylvia's place.

If his side wasn't so sore, he would have laughed out loud.

***

They are walking down the garden path. Behind them, Hannes closes the door.

"I still can't believe …" surmise Petrus, but his words freeze in his throat. Out of the corner of his eye, he sees the tiniest of movement of the shrub in the dim streetlight. Instinctively, he bumps Jasper out of the way while he dives to the side. As if in a dream, he hears the dull tjof from the silencer and then he feels a burning along his arm as the bullet tears through the sleeve of his jacket.

Another two shots follow, but the bullets are too high and hit the wall behind them. Now he can make out a faint figure coming out from behind the bush. Then a .38 bangs ear-deafening two times next to his head. He sees the figure' hands flying in the air.

"I've got him," Jaspers says drily while Petrus comes on his knees.

***

Petrus is sitting in the armchair in the sitting room. He wonders how many hours has he been awake. The sun is creeping over the horizon in light red glamour.

He hopes Hannes is safely on his way to Botswana.

His cell rings. It is Karin.

"Petrus, I've been trying for hours to get to you on your cell. I also tried the landline. I have been restless the whole night. It felt as if something dreadful happened to you. Is everything okay? I haven't slept a wink last night."

"Lovey, everything is fine. I haven't suffered something serious."

"If that is so, it means something happened."

He suddenly longs intensely to her.

"Nothing serious. Only a little scratch on my arm."

"Petrus!" He can hear the distress in her voice. Then calmer, she continues. "Petrus, I am sorry. I have suddenly become scared of losing you. Should I come home? I promise no more parties. You were right sending us to the farm. I have thought much about myself and our marriage. I love you, Petrus."

"Love you too, my darling."

In a soft voice, she whispers. "Only you and me and Stefan." She giggles. "Maybe a little sister for him?"

He scarcely can speak as his voice becomes thick of gladness and compassion.

"Don't come. I am going to shower and shave and put on clean clothes. See you in a few hours on the farm. Give Stefan a kiss from me."

He rises and go and stand in front of the big sitting room window and looks at the bright light of the rising sun.

His future is shining like the sun.

ABOUT THE AUTHOR

Gert van Jaarsveld is a retired professor in Linguistics after a successful academic career of 25 years. He also has years of experience in translation, editing, proofreading in English and Afrikaans. Since 2018 he is the editor and translator of the serials and other content in The Free Story Magazine. He also is a published author of short stories, novels and articles. His eBooks features in the Story Magazine's Bookshop.